She was dying for him

Every flick of Drew's tongue against her breast sent bolts of delight downward, until the throbbing between her legs became almost unbearable. Their lips met again in a hot, quick mating, and she reached for his belt.

When he leaned away, Tori whispered, "I want this," reassuring him as she reached for him again.

"Not now."

Tori froze, her fingers just barely brushing the front of his pants, where his visible erection strained against the fabric. "You want to run that by me again?"

He closed his eyes and gave one hard shake of his head. "God, if only you knew how hard this is for me...."

"It's *hard* for *me*," she said, staring at his crotch. "I can *see* how *hard* it is for *me*."

A hoarse laugh that sounded more pained than amused erupted from his lips. "You're not ready," he finally said.

Oh, she was ready, all right. "Wanna bet?" she snapped. Then she proved it to him by grabbing his hand and pulling it down her body. Down over the front of her jeans. And right between her legs, where the fabric was damp and hot.

"Any *more* questions?" she asked.

Dear Reader,

Is there anything hotter than a gorgeous man who's so intelligent he doesn't even realize how sexy he is? Not to me there isn't. I just love the kind of guy who's so secure in himself that the question of how he looks never even enters his mind.

Drew Bennett is just such a man. Brilliant, driven, cultured, worldly and intuitive, the last thing he's worried about is whether or not women are attracted to his brawny shoulders or brilliant blue eyes. He considers the mind so much more important.

Such a man definitely needs a wake-up call, don't you think? And Tori Lyons is about to give him one. Tori's known a lot of men. The drag-racing circuit is full of them. But she's never met one like Drew, and she's willing to do anything—even give herself a complete cultural makeover—to get his attention.

If you've read my August book, *Killing Time,* you know I love those reality shows. This one was such a ball to create. I really hope Tori and Drew...as well as all the rest of the crazy cast and crew...give you a few hours of reading pleasure.

Best wishes,

Leslie Kelly

Books by Leslie Kelly

LESLIE KELLY

Make Me Over

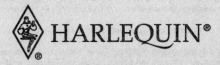

HARLEQUIN®

TORONTO • NEW YORK • LONDON
AMSTERDAM • PARIS • SYDNEY • HAMBURG
STOCKHOLM • ATHENS • TOKYO • MILAN • MADRID
PRAGUE • WARSAW • BUDAPEST • AUCKLAND

To all the members of my incredibly supportive
RWA chapters: CFRW, TARA and my home chapter,
FL-STAR. I appreciate you all more than you'll ever know.

ISBN 0-373-69204-8

MAKE ME OVER

Prologue

"IF YOU THINK I'm ever gonna work on the set of another reality TV show, you're whacked in the head, old man."

Jacey Turner stared at her father across his expansive desk in his highbrow Hollywood office, not believing he'd just asked her to take over as lead camera operator on his latest project. And definitely not believing *why* he was asking.

He was nearly broke. Burt Mueller, the king of TV in the 1970s, had backed a string of stinkers in more recent decades—everyone knew that. But she'd never thought he'd come to this. Losing his edge, his power, his "in"-ness.

Cripes…his *Rolls.*

"I'm serious. I need you, babe."

"Whacked," she continued, as if he hadn't spoken. "Or you've been popping some of those happy pills that got you through the sixties."

Daddy dearest tsked as he gestured toward his recently Botoxed face, which looked as if it belonged on a forty year old—not someone two decades older. "Do you think I'd spend *this* much money on trainers and plastic surgeons to go and poison myself with drugs?"

She cast a pointed look at the cigarette smoldering in the ashtray on his desk. Against policy in this no-smoking building, like every other building in L.A. these days. As if he cared.

Burt merely shrugged. "They're not hurting me on the *outside*, which is more important to me than my lungs right now."

God, how could a man say something so completely shallow, yet manage to make it sound so sincere? She couldn't help chuckling. "Tell that to the wrinkles that are eventually gonna show back up around your mouth from constantly having a cancer stick clamped between your lips."

"You berate me because you care."

Yeah, she did. And he knew it. Leaning back in the chair, she put her boot-clad feet on his desk and crossed them, just to keep him guessing. She did not need the old man realizing she'd do just about anything for him. "Okay, be honest, how bad could it be? I mean, the residuals on *Paw Come Git Your Dinner* alone should keep you in Bruno Magli shoes until you're ninety."

"You're thinking like a Hollywood insider of *today*. Not of the seventies," he retorted, sounding weary. "Residuals? Ha. Ask me why stars of *The Brady Bunch* made so many bad reunion movies, until I thought we might soon see *Alice Does Dallas*. Or why Gilligan's gang had to be rescued by the Harlem Globetrotters."

Jacey, who recognized the shows by their eternal life on TV Land, merely waited.

"It's so Gilligan doesn't have to shine shoes at LAX and Cindy, Jan and Marcia don't have to work as Hooters girls. Everything was in the studio's favor in those days."

Okay, she'd heard that, but still found it hard to believe Burt could be so bad off. She was looking at the man who'd created six of the top ten shows of 1970. Who'd first seized on canned laughter to beef up audience response and sparked a revolution in sitcoms. Who'd earned ten Emmys, for piss sake!

"So you really think you can salvage a historic thirty-some-years career as a TV legend by jumping on the reality-show hysteria which hasn't died its overdue death? What a dumb idea."

He didn't take offense. Her old man never took offense at anything, except being called a has-been. And he certainly didn't get all fatherly on her. Why would he? Their relationship wasn't like that. He hadn't even known she existed until she'd shown up on his doorstep at age seventeen with a ratty backpack and a bad attitude, informing him he was her dear old dad.

Some Hollywood types would've kicked her to the curb. Burt Mueller hadn't. He'd taken her in, welcomed her, convinced her he'd never known of her existence, and given her a job.

Somehow, over the past six years, they'd become, well, if not exactly what you'd call family…at least friends. But there was only so much she'd do for friendship. And setting foot on the set of another reality show wasn't on the list. Not after the last one, *Killing Time In A Small Town*, where she'd worked as lead camera operator. Because getting fired hadn't been the highlight of her frickin' year.

Though honestly, she had to admit, the experience hadn't been *all* bad. And the show had done *really* well in ratings this fall.

She also had to give thanks because of what it had led to in her personal life. She, tough-as-nails Jacey Turner, had let down her guard and fallen in love.

Lord, she missed Digg. Missed him like mad. But coming here to California to answer her father's desperate call wasn't such a bad thing. The past couple of months, when she and Digg had tried to make their unconventional romance work in the real world—*his* world of fire stations and big Hispanic-New York families—had been tough. Particularly because she suspected all of Digg's friends and loved ones secretly looked at her as a sewer rat who'd glommed on to him for the million bucks he'd won on *Killing Time*. She couldn't prove it, but she'd lay money his mother made the sign of the cross behind her back every time Jacey entered her house.

She'd been hiding her unhappiness at that—and at not being able to land a job with any studio in New York—for weeks now.

"It'll be a good break for you," Burt said, moving in for the kill. "A classy mansion in New England in the winter. Snow, skiing, hot chocolate."

"Gag me. I'm not an Aspen bunny. Remember? I skied on a skateboard in the aqueducts of South Central."

He chuckled. "Then do it because you need the money, too."

She raised a brow, but didn't ask how he knew. He knew everything. "What's this show about, anyway?"

He didn't gloat over being right, though he grinned as he filled her in. When he was done, she sighed. "Sounds boring. A social makeover show. Trashy girls get cash for class."

His brow shot indignantly up toward his bald head. "It's perfect. Like the musical, the one with Audrey Hepburn."

Jacey hated musicals. She could never get past how moronic a guy would look breaking out into a big song-and-dance number right in the middle of a gang war. If it happened in real life, someone would have Baker Acted the loser in two seconds flat. Those things made reality TV look realistic.

"You know the one," Burt continued. "He makes her over, she sings the song about how she coulda schtupped all night."

That made her snort a laugh, exactly as he'd intended. The old man was good. Because in spite of hating all musicals, she did have a soft spot for *one*. *My Fair Lady*. For the same reason she liked *Pretty Woman*. She enjoyed seeing the gutter girl fool all the rich snots into thinking she was all highbrow and stuff.

But she wouldn't give in so easily. "I still don't see the great angle. It's…ordinary."

Burt hated to be told that anything he touched could be ordinary. His scowl wasn't aimed at her, however; it was aimed at himself. Because even he had to see how dull the whole thing sounded. Put a bunch of uneducated girls in a house and teach them stuff. Whoop-de-fricking-wow.

"Well, *this* has certainly grabbed enough interest to land on the *Times* list," Burt finally said as he slid his rolling chair back and pulled a hardbound book off a shelf Jacey had assumed was merely for decoration. This book actually looked like it'd been opened. At least once.

She took it from him, studying the title. *Beyond Eliza Doolittle: Education vs. Genetics in Today's Society.* "Yawn."

"But it's not." Burt flipped the book over so she

could see the large black-and-white photo of the author on the back.

"Yum."

"Exactly. He's all the rage, and he's agreed to let us do a reality show based on the theories in this book, as long as we donate a large sum of money to educational charities."

Jacey hardly listened. She was too busy reading the bio on the author, Dr. Andrew Bennett. The bio didn't say much, but it revealed the most important detail. "He's single."

Burt tilted his head. "Interested?" The mild tone didn't fool her. He'd very much like to know what was going on with her love life. Heck, so would Jacey.

Shaking her head, she leaned back in her chair and crossed her arms, letting the creative juices really get flowing.

A fancy estate during the holidays. Bubbly hot tubs. Red wine in front of a fire. A bunch of busty bimbos in search of a little class-i-fication. And a hunky-as-heck brainiac doctor.

"I've got an idea," she finally said. "I think I just might have come up with a way for you to take this boring makeover show of yours and turn it into a *bona fide* hit."

Burt sat up straight, immediately interested. "How?"

"Well," Jacey replied smoothly, "it's simple. You don't make the women compete for money or to be named Grand Duchess of Poobah because her pinkie stays the highest during a tea party."

Her father huffed.

Leaning close to his desk, Jacey crossed her arms on its wood surface and met the old man's stare.

Once she was sure she had his complete attention, she tapped the photo on the back of the book with the tip of her nail.

"You make them compete for *him*."

1

He'd stumbled into a hooker convention.

Arriving at the Vermont estate to which he'd been directed, Dr. Andrew Bennett immediately suspected he'd made a wrong turn somewhere. Because this *had* to be a group of hookers raucously making themselves at home in the tastefully decorated library of a fabulous New England mansion. Either that or someone was filming an episode of *Girls Gone Wild*.

From the two brunettes and the redhead sitting on top of the bar doing shots—to the trio of blondes dirty dancing around a hapless waiter serving hors d'oeuvres—to the tall one lying on her back in the middle of the floor attempting to guzzle a yard of beer—to the petite, washed-out girl demonstrating pole dancing against the floor lamp, every woman in the room looked about as raucous, uncouth and outrageous as could be.

He'd asked for women with little education or social skills. Not the entire mud-wrestling team from Big Al's Slaughterhouse in Bangor.

Drew wished he felt elated to have such *raw* material to work with.

He didn't.

He wished he could muster some enthusiasm

about the daunting task of overseeing the transformation of these, er, *ladies* of the evening into real ladies.

He couldn't.

He wished he'd turned around and left the minute he'd seen two of the women competing in a spitting contest into the fireplace.

He hadn't.

He wished there was some legitimate reason he actually *had* to participate in this reality-show nonsense, rather than just let his book be the basis for it.

There wasn't.

He wished he could change his mind.

Too late. He was stuck. Here. With the rollicking house full of…test subjects.

One-on-one he could have handled. Frankly, he would have relished the opportunity to show the world what he'd learned from his own research…from his own life. Genetics or upbringing didn't determine the capacity of a person's success. Education did.

Education. Resilience. A modicum of social ability…they could overcome nearly any hurdles mere birth could bestow. Hadn't his transition from homeless kid of a flighty mother to college professor illustrated as much? God knew, if he, Drew Bennett—former thief and con artist who'd once picked pockets in Miami Beach to feed his kid sister—could make it from the back seat of an ancient, rusty VW Beetle to the podiums of Georgetown University, anyone could.

A crash jerked his attention back to the women in the room.

"Wooo, girl, you're gonna have to pay for that!" someone shouted as a redhead giggled over the vase she'd just knocked off an end table.

"Maybe they'll take it out in trade," the pole dancer said, sounding weary and jaded.

Drew blew out a long, frustrated breath.

Why he'd ever thought this reality-show idea might actually do some good, he had no idea. Back in September when he'd first been approached by the TV people, he'd refused. Not only because it seemed a silly idea, but also because he simply didn't have the time to deal with such nonsense. He'd already had to take the semester off teaching anthropology and sociology at Georgetown because of the insanity of book tours and publicity associated with being an overnight bestseller. Throw in his next project—a trip to a university in Mexico to participate in an expedition to an ancient Mayan city—and he was completely booked.

Then they'd hit him in his weak spot, his Achilles' heel. The production company had offered to donate ten percent of the *gross* profits of the show—not *net* profits; even he, a total non-Hollywood type knew better than that—to A Book and a Dream, Drew's favorite charity. Few people knew Drew had helped found the organization, which taught reading to underprivileged kids. That they'd investigated him enough to track down the information showed how serious they were.

The biggest hitch came when they'd suddenly decided, last week, that *he* had to be on the set to oversee things and gauge the women's progress. But when the ten percent had gone up to fifteen, he'd allowed himself to be persuaded. He'd consoled himself over the decision by thinking it wouldn't be *that* difficult. He could transform anyone who had the drive and basic intelligence to succeed.

But not a dozen women at once.

Certainly not *these* dozen women, who looked much more up for a rave than a grammar lesson.

Sighing heavily, he turned to leave, thankful no one had spotted him, when suddenly his attention was caught by one woman who stood apart from the rest. Her back to the room, she faced a floor-to-ceiling bookcase loaded with leather-bound editions, completely oblivious to the cacophony behind her. She remained separate. Distinct. In a bubble of introspection over the books—a posture Drew could understand, having lost himself in research on many occasions.

From behind, she was, well, to put it in the most basic terms…hot. She was petite, likely the smallest woman here. Tight, worn jeans clung to a slim pair of legs and a quite delectable backside. They nipped in to hug a tiny waist, though not without spreading over some fine curvy hips.

Her heavy, red flannel shirt was too bulky to allow him to make out much of the rest of her figure. But the thick bunch of wavy brown hair cascading down to the middle of her back led him to suspect she had brown eyes and olive skin.

Suddenly, the most unusual sensation drew his attention to his hands. Prickly. They tingled—though not from cold. He soon realized why. His mind was overflowing with images of twining his hands in all that hair, testing its weight, its silkiness.

It was not his *intellect* that decided she was most likely sexier than anyone he'd ever known. That intuitive response had come from somewhere south of his brain. South of his belt, to be precise.

Turn around.

She didn't respond to his silent order, leaving him wondering about the face of the woman who seemed so separate from the rest of the group.

"Woo hoo! Look who's here! Hold me back, ladies, but hands off 'cause he's mine."

Blinking, he tried to pull his focus off the woman by the bookcase, who continued to run her fingertip down the spines of several books as she read their titles. The fifteen or so others had stopped their various lewd and possibly illegal activities and had focused every bit of their attention on him. Every pair of eyes in the place widened in stares that ranged from friendly to voracious. He managed to remain completely still under the scrutiny, though he suddenly began to empathize with those guys who stripped off their clothes for women in trendy nightclubs.

"Come join the party, sweetie," the one on the floor said, a bit of beer dribbling down the side of her face. Wiping it off with the back of her hand, she gave him a big smile.

"Yeah, don't be shy," said the pole dancer, who suddenly looked much more animated. Like a tigress confronting a wounded wildebeest.

"Don't mind me, ladies," Drew murmured, nodding to them all. "I'm simply here to observe."

A flurry of protests broke out from the women, all of whom were giving him lascivious looks usually found during mating rituals. Not in New England mansions.

He pulled back slightly, deciding he needed to track down Burt Mueller, or whoever was in charge, and try to end this thing here and now. Frankly, he'd rather be back in Bolivia searching for evidence of the ancient lost civilization of the Bodomoqua tribe—while dodging armed guerrillas and the military—than spend an hour in this place.

Before he could exit, however, something came flying through the air from the group at the bar. He tried to duck, to no avail. The thing landed right on his head, dangling down to block his vision, and he blinked in response.

It took less than a second to realize exactly what he was looking at: a pair of black-and-red thong underwear.

And suddenly, because the thing rested right against his face with nothing to cover his eyes, Dr. Drew Bennett wished one more thing.

That he'd been wearing his glasses instead of his contacts.

IF SHE LIVED TO BE a hundred, Tori Lyons was never gonna make another deathbed promise. Specially to somebody who up and got better afterward. Seemed to her if you didn't die, all bets should be off. Promises, too.

Not that she wasn't happy Daddy had recovered from the heart attack that had about given them *all* heart attacks last September. She was. She thanked the Lord and all his little angels for his full recovery. Now, just three months later, he was back to his cantankerous self, on and off the track.

But she hadn't counted on him holding her to her promise: to get some education. Criminy, when she'd made the durn promise, she'd figured he meant for her to take some shop courses at the tech school near home in Sheets Creek, Tennessee.

'Course, at the time, in the exam room of Doc Barnes's vet clinic—where they'd taken Daddy on account of the closest hospital was forty miles away—she'd figured she might not have to go through with it. In the back of her mind, over the sound of Aunt Teeny wailin' for Jesus to spare her brother, and Daddy's girlfriend of fifteen years tellin' him she'd skin him like a polecat if he died before he got around to marryin' her, she'd figured it was a long shot. Because what high-tech school like Rudy B's Garage of Higher Learnin' would have *her,* a high-school dropout who'd only taken her GED two years ago 'cause it was the only way she could get her youngest brother to take it?

She'd passed. He hadn't. Huh. Go figure.

Still, she'd made the promise, which she'da kept, if she'd been able to. Would've been a waste of time, of course. Tori'd been learning her trade since the age of five in the pits and garages of drag strips across America. Wasn't much she couldn't do with a torque wrench or a transmission. Or an engine that only ran the quarter mile in six seconds at Talladega and needed to be under 5.6 by Music City.

But yessir, she woulda tried to keep her promise to her dear old departed daddy.

Only, the stubborn old cuss hadn't departed. And to add insult to injury, he'd held her to her promise. Tori'd given in, if only so Daddy'd get some peace of mind knowin' that when he finally *did* go to meet Jesus, he could be sure his kin on earth were doin' what he wanted them to.

Just like they'd always done when he was alive.

She'd been fixin' to start up in mechanic's class come January. But noooooo, Daddy'd had some high-falutin educatin' in mind. It was her bad luck that he'd run into some fella in Kentucky who was lookin' for girls to be part of a big makeover thingamabob.

Which was how she'd ended up here. On the set of a hoity-toity, high-class reality TV show. When she should be home, not only helpin' Daddy get back onto the NHRA—National Hot Rod Association—circuit, but also gearin' up for Christmastime in Sheets Creek.

He'd never've asked one of her spoiled rotten brothers to do somethin' so senseless. Then she scowled, the thought of her middle brother, Luther, makin' her fingers curl up into fists. She'd like to land one of them on his fat nose.

The phone call she'd had from him last night at the hotel in Albany had repeated in her brain all night long. Stupid Luther and his stupid bettin'. That boy was too poor to pay attention, but he'd been runnin' with the big dogs out at the track. He'd really done himself in this time and had told Tori she *had* to win on the show to come up with enough money to bail him out of his troubles.

Not durn likely. She was gettin' outta here first thing tomorrow and headin' home to whack some sense into him, then to figure out a way to pay off his debt. Because the money she could earn if she stuck it all the way out to the end of this here reality-show thing *still* wouldn't be enough to pay off Joe-Bob Baker, the toughest bookie in Knoxville.

What Luther didn't know was that the big prize on *Hey, Make Me Over* was a shopping spree for clothes and stuff. And to get all gussied up and go to some nose-in-the-air Christmas Eve party in New York City. As if she really wanted to go to a party— on Christmas no less—with the highfalutin folks who, right now, wouldn't spit on her if she was afire.

No, she needed to get outta here. Fast. Then she'd find a way to get the money to keep her ornery brother alive all right. At least long enough for her to whale on him like a rented mule. An ass-whuppin' was gonna come along with her help, that was for sure. The thought cheered her right up.

"Good evening, ladies, if you're finished with cocktail hour, perhaps you'd care to follow me to the dining room."

She looked up at the squeaky little butler, who was dressed like a penguin and looked stiff enough to have been dipped in shellac. His nose was always quiverin', like he'd caught a whiff of something rank. Put her right on edge.

Jiminy crickets, she didn't belong here. Not with a pushy butler, and cameras everywhere and expensive furniture that looked like it'd break if you took a real sit-down on it. Nossir, she was as out of place as a skunk at a garden party.

Except, she had to admit, with all the *other* women in the room. With them, she almost felt right at home.

"Whadda I gotta do to get myself kicked offa this thing fast?" she said under her breath.

One of the other contestants, a redhead named Sukie, replied, "Pick your nose at dinner."

Sukie and Tori had struck up a quick friendship when they'd arrived earlier today at this mansion in Vermont. Probably because the two of them had been so tickled by the way the butler came back every time one of 'em gave a pull on that cloth rope in the corner. Sukie and Tori had pulled the rope about twenty times today, until she thought Mr. Shellac was gonna take a pair of scissors to the thing.

Or to her and Sukie.

"I gotta be the first one gone, but I grew up watchin' my granddaddy dig for nose gold at the dinner table, and I don't think I could do it," Tori said. "There's gotta be another way."

"You'll think of something," said Sukie with a loud smack of her shiny pink bubblegum.

Sukie worked as a hairdresser in Cleveland and was so far Tori's favorite to win the grand prize. Anybody who could walk in those fancy, glittery four-inch-tall heels had the makins' of a real lady.

Blowing a big, juicy bubble and cracking it between her teeth, Sukie added, "And if you don't, you can always scratch yourself or start a food fight tomorrow. Tonight doesn't count, anyway."

Tori was glad've that much. Tonight was just a social gathering, a get-to-know-you party before taping got started tomorrow. So there wouldn't be no pressure to compete with anybody else, or time to worry where the cameras were hidden. But Tori believed in getting a head start. It was never too soon to make a bad impression.

Trouble was, she greatly feared even nose pickin' wasn't gonna make her stand out in this crowd, which included a trucker, a bartender—she'd been working the bar and, from the sound of it, making some wicked good hurricanes—some sales clerks, a stripper or two, a maid, and one girl named Ginny who had a huge set of knockers, which she'd gladly flashed at anyone they'd passed during the bus trip up from Albany.

"You don't really wanna leave already, do you?" asked Sukie as they turned to follow the other women—and the penguin—into the dining room.

"I sure do," Tori said. "I had to come 'cause I

promised my daddy. That don't mean I gotta stay. If I get throwed off, he can't never say I didn't try."

And then I'll have time to figure out how to help Luther.

Then she sighed. Because truly, she wasn't sure of the best way to get tossed out—by being too bad…or by being too good? The fast-talkin' producer, Mr. Mueller, might be looking for girls who were the *worst* off to keep around. Making it funner for the TV folks. After all, Tori, herself, liked watching the real stinkeroos on *American Idol.*

But, since the whole show was supposed to be about one girl gettin' lots of class and manners and going to the society party in New York, they might be lookin' for the girls most likely to pull it off. Meaning they'd want the ones who were the *best* of the bunch.

So the question remained: should she be on her best behavior? Or her worst?

"I wouldn't mind staying if I get to find out who the hunky guy who got a face-full of Ginny's panties was."

Tori scrunched up her brow, not knowing what the other woman meant.

"You were staring at the books like none of us were even in the room," Sukie said. "And ooh, girl, what you missed! A hunka burning love standing in the doorway, all tall and sexy and looking like he stepped right off an underwear billboard."

"He was in his underwear?" Tori squeaked.

"Nuh-uh. I was imagining."

Tori frowned. "He got a pair of used drawers on his face?"

Sukie shook her head. "Ginny pulled 'em outta her pocket."

Tori didn't rightly wanna know why somebody

carried underdrawers in their pocket. But since Ginny hadn't minded showin' every driver on the interstate her hooters, maybe she didn't go around wearin' her underwear, either, and just had 'em stashed nearby for emergencies. Like, hmm…goin' to church or climbin' a ladder or somethin'.

Before she could ask any more questions, they all had to leave to follow the butler through the maze of halls. Shew, she'd seen hotels smaller than this place. More welcomin' too. Christmas was three weeks from today, but there wasn't one pretty red bow or as much as a sprig of holly in sight.

Christmas was Tori's favorite time of year. And she sure didn't wanna spend it in *this* place that was about as friendly as a huntin' dog with a burr up its butt. That made her even more sure she wanted to get herself thrown outta here as soon as possible.

To her surprise, dinner was a hoot. Much more fun than she'd ever expected. The girls had a ball squawkin' over the nasty stuff put in front of them. Finally, after all of them had downright refused to so much as *taste* the slimy-looking snails they'd been served, they got somethin' normal. Steak 'n' potatoes. It wasn't Granny Lyons's fried catfish, but it stuck to the ribs all right.

She had figured somebody official from the show would come and talk to them tonight, but the butler said they had the evening all free and clear to themselves. And tomorrow bright and early things'd get underway. So after dinner they were on their own.

Most everyone went to the game room or the fancy in-house theater, where somebody said they was gonna watch *Days of Thunder*. Tori'd seen that movie nigh on a hundred times, always wonderin' if drivers who looked like Tom Cruise really were on the NASCAR circuit—since they sure weren't on the NHRA. So she passed on the movie. Instead, she moseyed on through the quiet house, tiptoein' like, because she didn't want to bump into anybody. She wasn't gonna steal nothin', she just wanted to be alone. To enjoy the one thing about this place she might actually miss once she got herself thrown outta here tomorrow.

The library.

Shew-ee the room was full, floor to ceilin', of bookcases. She'd never seen so many books in one place in her life. The only library Sheets Creek had was one'a them books-on-wheels trucks. Since the donated truck had once been driven by the ice cream man—an' still had the faintest smell of fudge pops on a hot summer day—it attracted the attention of a lot of dogs when it drove down the street. Not to mention the young 'uns who came scramblin' outside with their pennies and nickels, only to pitch rocks at the tires when they found out the driver had books and magazines, not fudgies and Sno-Kones.

Tori watched for the library truck though, since it was a good way to practice up on her readin'. She wasn't very good at it, but she sure did like it. Usually the truck only had picture books for the kids or magazines that'd been handled so much it'd make your fingers greasy to touch one. Tori didn't care. She gobbled up whatever she could find.

Only she'd never seen *nothin'* like this place. Rows and rows of shelves, all of 'em with nice pretty books…hardcover books without cracked spines or yellowed dog-eared pages. Ones that hadn't been handled by half the population of Kruger County.

Keeping the lights low, just in case the butler had been funnin' them about no cameras being in use tonight, Tori made her way to the shelf she'd been starin' at earlier. She pulled down the exact book she wanted...*Tom Sawyer,* and turned around to curl up on one of the leather couches.

"I see we had the same idea."

The voice startled her so much, she nearly dropped the book.

"I'm sorry, I didn't mean to frighten you."

A lamp on one of the rickety little tables clicked on, and Tori saw who'd been talkin' in the dim light.

A man. A holy-moly-save-us-Mary-and-all-the-saints gorgeous-lookin' man. He took her breath away, making it hard to even breathe, much less talk.

He had hair so dark it looked like fresh-laid blacktop. Thick and shiny with a bit of wave. Dark brown eyes stared at her from a face that looked like it should be on a movie screen. Lean cheeks, strong jaw, lips just the right size for suckin' on during a long, hot night of lovin'.

Please let the rest of him match, she whispered mentally before looking down. She almost sighed in relief, because the rest of him was as pretty as the top. All tall and lean. Not thick and bulky like so many of the boys she knew back home, who liked to get together and throw tree stumps to see who was strongest. The bulk'd turn to fat in five years, once those boys settled down.

No, this man was nothin' like that. He was perfect and sexy and hotter 'n Satan's housecoat.

And starin'.

With one of *those* stares. The kind men had been givin' her since she turned fourteen or so and started gettin' all bumpy under her jeans and baggy shirts. Hungry like.

Only, this time, for the first time in her whole entire twenty-three years, Tori felt ravenous-hungry, too.

2

DREW COULDN'T STOP STARING at the young woman who'd crept in here so quietly he hadn't even realized she was here until she'd taken a book from the shelf. It was the brunette he'd been so captivated by earlier. He could tell by the jeans and red flannel shirt. Not to mention the long curly hair that rioted around one of the prettiest faces he'd ever seen.

He'd been wrong about one thing. Her eyes weren't brown. They were blue. Deep, beautiful blue, surrounded by thick, black lashes. And as he stared into them, he felt something shift.

The earth beneath his feet, maybe. Or just his perception of it.

She watched him warily from a few feet away, saying nothing, her eyes wide and her lips parted as she drew in deep, even breaths. He half wondered if she was about to flee. Because she looked...hesitant. As if waiting for something.

"I guess we both needed to get away from the madness for a little while, hmm?" he finally managed to say.

She nodded.

A conversationalist she was not, leaving him more confused about who she was. It seemed impossible that she could be one of the women here to participate in the show. Because, though dressed casually, she'd seemed so very distant from the rest of the contestants earlier. Above it all, somehow, not even deigning to turn around when he'd been so raucously discovered.

And now, from the tilt of her pert chin to the sharp intelligence shining through those amazing blue eyes, she seemed already perfect. Certainly not in need of any improvement on a ridiculous reality show.

"Where is everyone else?"

She merely shrugged.

He tried again. "What book did you decide on?"

She held it up and stepped closer, then closer, until she stood only a foot away. He was able to make out the title in the semidarkness of the room.

More importantly, he could make out every feature on her face, every freckle, the sparkle of gold on the tips of her hair. And he could feel her warm breaths touching his skin, and her clean, flowery scent filling his head so he could barely think.

He stared at her for a long moment, asking a million questions. Who she was. Where she was from.

Exactly how long she needed to know a man before she'd allow him to take her to bed.

Shaking off his momentary lapse into insanity— not to mention bad manners—he focused on the book. "Tom Sawyer." Clearing his throat, he added, "That's a good one."

She simply nodded.

Finally, crossing his arms, he peered down at her curiously. "Are you unable to speak?"

This time he got a shake of the head in response.

He had to chuckle. "Was that a no, you're not *unable* to speak? Or a no you can't speak?"

"I can," she whispered.

"Then why aren't you?"

She blew out an impatient breath and rolled her eyes. "Because I was hopin' if I kept quiet, you'd shut up, too, and get back to lookin' at me the way you was a minute ago."

Eyes growing wide, Drew just stared at her for a moment. The young woman was practically glaring at him, so her heavily twanged words didn't quite sink in. "Excuse me?"

"I said…"

"I heard you."

"So why'd you 'scuse yourself?" Then she nibbled her lip. "Oh, did you, uh, make a noise or somethin'?"

Startled into a laugh, Drew shook his head. "I'm sorry, maybe we should start this conversation again. Okay?"

"I guess."

"Hello," Drew said, extending his hand to shake hers. "I'm Drew Bennett."

She stared at his hand for a moment. Finally she extended her own, grasping his so hard he felt like he was meeting a linebacker. "Tori Lyons."

"A pleasure to meet you, Tori."

"Likewise."

"Now," Drew said, getting back to her original comment, "why did you want me to shut up?"

She visibly swallowed, then slipped her tongue out to moisten her pretty pink lips. An uncalculated move, it still hit him hard, somewhere down low, bringing forth a reaction that had everything to do with instinct and nothing to do with intellect.

"You was starin'," she finally replied, her voice husky.

"Yes."

She hesitated, then tilted her head back in challenge. "I kinda liked it."

"You liked me staring at you?"

"The *way* you was starin'."

"Were staring," he couldn't help murmuring. "Why?"

She raised one brow, giving him a look that dared him to deny he'd been looking at her with a great deal of visceral appreciation. He wouldn't deny any such thing. He just wanted to know why she'd...*liked* it.

"You was lookin' at me like you was a hound dog and me a rare, juicy steak."

Being compared to a hound dog amused him. Considering his primitive response to her, he probably deserved the comparison. "Perhaps I was. I beg your pardon."

"For what? You make another noise?"

"No, I beg your pardon for staring."

"I toldja I liked it. Kinda took me by surprise, because usually when a man stares at me like that, I wanna black his eye."

Considering the top of her head barely reached his chin, he questioned whether she'd be able to reach his eye. But he didn't want to tempt fate by asking her. "Well, you're correct. I was staring. My apologies. Your appearance here took *me* by surprise." Seeing she wouldn't buy that simple of an explanation, he admitted, "And you're very pretty."

"Thankee," she said with a tiny smile and a tinier nod. "So're you."

"So are," he murmured, even as he smiled inwardly at being called pretty.

"So are what?"

He realized he'd once again corrected her, not even realizing he was doing it. The teacher in him was easing in on this conversation, taking over for the hound dog. Not surprising, probably. Judging by her speech, she was, indeed, a contestant on this reality show. Meaning, his pupil.

He nearly groaned at the realization. Because this was not a woman he could pursue, by any means. So far, he'd gone through his entire professional career without ever even being tempted by a student. And he'd sworn he never would.

Which just about killed him since his whole body was still tight with the awareness of her sweet scent and soft breaths. Her heart-shaped face. That hair.

He quickly changed the subject. "Can I assume you're here for the, uh, reality show?"

Almost grunting her response, she plopped down onto the leather sofa, where Drew had been sitting until she'd arrived. "Ayuh."

He sat down beside her, not too close—not trusting himself to get within touching distance of her. His thoughts were too jumbled, his emotions too sharp as he spoke to this unusual young woman for him to risk physical closeness.

The wise thing, given his instant attraction to her from the moment he'd seen her earlier, would be to leave. Immediately. To go to his room and think about whether Burt Mueller had really meant it when he said he'd pull the plug on the whole show—and the charitable donation—if Drew didn't stay to participate.

Something, however, kept him here, in the secluded darkness of the quiet room, where he could hear nothing more than the soft tick of a mantel clock and her even softer breaths.

"You don't seem too happy about being on television," he murmured.

"How'd you like ta be a lab rat?"

Interesting. She wasn't here by choice. "So why did you come?"

"Deathbed promise."

He gave her a sympathetic look. "I'm sorry."

"For what?"

"That someone died. Someone you cared about?"

"He didn't die, the stubborn ole mule. But he held me to the promise anyway. Weren't fair."

"*Wasn't* fair."

"Do you know you keep repeatin' everything I say?" she asked. Then she leaned forward, dropping her hand on his knee. The contact was innocent, yet made warmth explode upward from there, flooding his whole body with awareness of her touch.

"If you got a problem or somethin', you know, with your talkin', that's okay. I've known people who repeated everything twice. 'Course, they was old… or, like my aunt Millie, they'd got kicked in the head by a mule or somethin'." Then she frowned in concentration. "No, come to think of it, Aunt Millie *always* repeats herself, on account of her havin' so many kids in her family nobody'd ever listen to her." Then she smiled. "I remember now. The time she got kicked in the head, she just started talkin' in Latin. Took her fallin' off the porch a few weeks later to get her speakin' natural again."

Amused by her story—and the way she told it—he could only grin at her. "You mean someone you know really began to speak a foreign language after a head injury?"

"Heck, pig latin ain't foreign t'anybody," she said with a snicker. "Every five year old knows it."

Pig latin. He sucked his lips into his mouth to prevent a laugh, liking her down-home humor more and more. "I'm sorry I've been repeating your words. I was automatically trying to correct your grammar."

"You a teacher or somethin'?"

He nodded.

"For real? I figured you was one'a them TV folks."

"I teach anthropology and sociology at Georgetown University in Washington."

She snorted. "Sociology?"

He nodded.

"Jiminy crickets, they got college classes for everything these days, don't they? As if a body needs to learn how to be sociable. Down in Sheets Creek, bein' sociable's about second nature, since neighbors gotta rely on each other most times."

"Sheets Creek?" he asked, more interested in where she was from than in explaining the much more boring details of his job.

"Tennessee. It's a teeny town, twenty miles from the nearest grocery store. There's a little shop inside the gas station for emergencies, but you can't never be sure if you're buyin' somethin' that's fresh or that's been settin' there for five years. So you gotta be sociable with your neighbors, because, if'n you run outta flour or sugar you sure don't wanna have to make a twenty mile trek right in the middle of baking day."

"I see. Do you like living there?"

She shrugged, glancing away, not meeting his eye directly for the first time since they'd sat down. "I s'pose. I get to travel a lot, so it's not like I ain't never seen the rest of the world."

"Not like *I've never* seen the rest of the world."

"You travel a lot, too?" Groaning, she shot him a glare. "Stop doin' that teacher stuff on me."

"I'm sorry, Tori, I don't mean to. It's…instinctual." Then he clarified. "Habit."

"I know what instinctual is," she retorted. "I ain't ignorant. It's like the way tub-a-guts Bubba Freeman always sucks in his belly and sticks out his chest whenever a pretty girl walks into the garage, even though that boy not only fell outta the ugly tree, he got beat on by the whole forest."

He supposed the analogy worked.

"Now, you were saying you've seen the world?" he asked.

She leaned back on the sofa, lifting her boot-clad feet to rest them on the coffee table. "Well, mosta the US of A below the Mason-Dixon line. I been ridin' the southern circuit with my daddy and my brothers for nigh on twelve years now, since Mama died."

"I'm sorry."

This time, she didn't question him. A brief nod acknowledged his expression of sympathy. "Daddy's driven in a few national races, so I even been as far away as San Diego, California."

"Races? Is your father a race-car driver?"

She nodded.

"And you…"

"I'm head of his pit crew. And a backup driver."

His jaw dropped in surprise. This tiny, lovely looking woman was a mechanic and a race-car driver? "You're serious?"

She giggled at his look of surprise.

"You drive small cars at high rates of speed on an enclosed track for hundreds of miles?" he asked, still trying to get his mind around it.

"Nope. NHRA." When he simply stared, she explained, "Hot rods." When he still didn't understand, she sighed deeply. "Drag racing. Not long distances, it's quarter mile. Get it?"

When he finally nodded, still speechless, she added, "Daddy's one of the top funny car drivers in the country."

Drag racing. So she drove even smaller cars, at even shorter distances...at even higher speeds. Somehow, that didn't make him feel better. "And your father—is he the one who elicited your promise to come here?"

"If your askin' did he use some chest pains to get me to agree to get some higher learnin', yeah, he'd be the one all right."

Higher learning. On the set of a reality-television show. He didn't begin to have the time to evaluate that contradiction.

Though he didn't ask, Tori must have seen the curiosity in his expression. Because she began explaining her sport to him, the history, the importance of air velocity and starting speed.

But all he could think about was her little body inside a tiny metal can hurtling at over two hundred miles per hour.

"Do your brothers work with your father, too?"

She snorted. "Not hardly what you'd call work. My oldest younger brother, Jimmy, he was backup driver, 'til he got hitched last year. His wife put her foot down about him bein' gone so much, what with her 'n' their three kids at home."

He didn't so much as bat an eye.

"My baby brother, Sammy, he works the crew, but he's pretty green still. More interested in chasin' the track hos than payin' attention to the art of draggin'."

Didn't bat one at that, either. He just smiled inwardly, liking her voice, the way she softened her words with that Tennessee twang. He also liked what she revealed about herself—her life, how hard she worked, her enthusiasm for her job—with every word she spoke.

"As for Luther…" This time, her whole body grew tense. Her fingers curled into fists in her lap, and Drew suddenly wondered exactly what poor Luther had done to inspire such anger in his sister. But she didn't elaborate. "Well, he's about as useless as tits on a boar hog around cars."

How…colorful. Still, a clear description. He began to understand her enmity toward her lazy brother Luther. "So you're your daddy's heir?"

She met his eye and nodded slowly. "I suppose."

Hearing the slight hesitation in her voice, he had to ask, "How do you feel about that? Is it what you'd choose for yourself, if you had a choice?"

Her gaze returned to her lap, where her fingers remained tightly clenched. "Sure."

She was lying. But he wasn't going to be rude enough to call her on it. "You're the oldest, with three younger brothers. No sisters?"

"Huh-uh. Jimmy's one year younger than me, Luther one year younger than him, and Sammy one step more. Except, three days outta the year, Sammy's the same age as Luther, because their birthdays are only three days apart." Then she shrugged. "We all have October birthdays, on account of January being cold. And it bein' off-season so Daddy didn't have nothin' better to do than be botherin' Mama."

It took him a second, but he got it. He couldn't help laughing. The fondness in her smile as she laughed along told him a lot about how she felt toward her family.

"You miss them."

She nodded. "But it won't be for long. I plan on skedaddlin' outta here tomorrow. Next day at the latest."

He stiffened suddenly, as the word *no* flashed through his brain. "You can't. The show…"

"Girls start gettin' kicked off tomorrow. I aim to be the first."

He couldn't explain the dismay that swept through him at her words. He'd only known her a short time, but he'd already realized something very important. Tori could be the one. She could be exactly the woman Burt Mueller—and he, Drew Bennett— had been looking for.

She was lovely and sweet. Funny and quick-witted. Her lack of education didn't diminish one bit from what he sensed was real intelligence behind her pretty blue eyes. And her spirit and tenacity hinted she would give herself wholeheartedly to something once she'd set her mind to do it.

Why she'd set her mind to leaving, he had no idea. But one thing was sure. He'd do *anything* to get her to stay.

TORI'D BEEN JABBERIN' ON about her life and her family and drivin' for over an hour, and she still couldn't focus on much besides the mouth of the man she was talkin' to.

She wanted to kiss Drew Bennett. To kiss him and kiss him and never stop. Well, maybe stop a little, so she could look up at him and see him starin' at her in the hungry way he had right at first. She'd been ogled by men from time to time. But that didn't feel nothin' like the warm, tingly way this handsome man had made her feel.

Not only handsome, he was also nice and smart and he smelled like somethin' salty and fresh. Like the ocean. He had the cutest little dent in his cheek when he laughed, and he listened real good, like he was interested in every word she had to say. And through it all, his dark eyes didn't hide what he was really thinkin'.

The same thing she was…about gettin' a *whole* lot closer.

He wanted her, too. Wanted her bad. There was only one reason he hadn't tried kissin' her yet and it had nothin' to do with her.

It was the show. This stupid reality show. There didn't seem to be no doubt he was here as some kind of teacher and that'd made him get all teacherly.

Shew-ee, if she'd ever had a English teacher who looked like this one, she mighta stuck it out for the rest of high school, insteada droppin' out when the readin' got too tough in junior year.

"You know," he said, after they'd been sittin' there in the near dark, jawin' for almost an hour, "I'm afraid you didn't get a chance to do much reading."

She shrugged. "Slow's I read, I'd probably still be on the second page, anyway."

He tilted his head and gave her one of the funny, intense-looking stares that made her go all a-quivery down in her belly. Like he wanted to crawl right inside her mind and settle down for a spell, gettin' to know all her secrets.

Well, she didn't want nobody inside her mind. But this here was one man she could honestly say she wouldn't mind havin' inside her body.

"Do you have trouble reading, Tori?"

"What?" she mumbled, havin' a hard time keeping up with the words when her mind was filled with all kinds of wicked pictures. Drew's mouth on hers. His hands windin' in her hair. His chest... Lord almighty, that body. Strippin' every piece of clothing off, down to his Skivvies.

"Wait," she said, snapping upright. "Are you the underwear man?"

His jaw about hit his chest it dropped so hard. Tori scrunched her eyes shut in embarrassment. "Sorry, I didn't mean that. I mean, Sukie, one of the girls, she said a steamin' hunka man came in here earlier and got a pair of drawers thrown at him."

The man turned red. Blushed like a bride on her weddin' day. The sight made Tori grin.

"I thought I'd stumbled into a hooker convention," he muttered.

"With a pair of undies on your head, I can see why."

"I don't suppose they were yours?" He sounded almost hopeful.

"Nope. I didn't even know you was in the room."

"No, you were busy looking at the books."

That she had been. Imagine how different her dinner mighta been if she'd had Drew's handsome face to think on, instead of focusin' on the sliminess of the snails on her plate. He was a lot more appetizin' than *anything* they coulda served in this place.

How she could've missed him in the room, she

had no idea. Them books must have spelled her or somethin'. Then she thought about what Ginny'd done, and how *she'd* feel havin' a pair of undies on her head. "They weren't used," she said, hoping that'd make him feel better. "In case you were, you know…wonderin'."

"Excuse me?"

This time, she knew what he meant, but gave him a saucy grin, anyways. "Another noise?"

"Tori…"

"I was just joshin'. I mean, Ginny, the girl who threw the scanties, she didn't pull 'em off herself or nothin'."

"Thank heaven for small favors."

"She pulled 'em outta her pocket." She grimaced. "I been tryin' to think why somebody'd need spare drawers in her pocket."

"Perhaps she was afraid her luggage would get lost."

He said it in so dry a voice, she knew right away he was funnin'. She chuckled, likin' this man's delivery. "Maybe." Then, thinkin' on it, she added, "I got a cousin who'll shimmy outta hers right under her dress and toss 'em to her boyfriend whenever she wants him to hurry up and take her home from the bar." Then she shrugged. "'Course, that's only when she's walkin' on a slant. She's a good girl when she ain't drinkin'. Works as one'a them cosmetologists puttin' makeup on the dead people down at Franklin's Funerals and Exterminatin'."

Drew just shook his head, a cute hunk of hair floppin' down onto his forehead. "Did you say a funeral parlor *and* exterminator?"

"Sheets Creek's kinda small," she explained. "Not

much buryin' business around, but they sure is a lotta bugs. So when he ain't haulin' a body around, ole Mr. Franklin hitches up a sprayer onto the back of his hearse."

Drew nodded. "You know, I think I might someday have to make a visit to Sheets Creek. It sounds as interesting as many of the ancient civilizations and societies I've studied."

It did? Shew, Tori figured Sheets Creek was about as normal and boring as any other town in America. Then she thought on the word he'd used. "Society," she repeated, soundin' it out, thinkin' on what he'd said earlier about his job. "That have somethin' to do with…what was the word you used…sociology?"

A little twinkle in his eye told her she was right.

Tori wanted to sink right through the couch onto the floor. She musta sounded like a fool prattling on about people bein' social. He didn't teach nothin' as dumb as how to get along with people. He taught about history and stuff. People from the past. Like them disco dancers from the seventies.

But Drew quickly distracted her from her fit of embarrassment. He reached over and put his hand on hers, until, suddenly, Tori couldn't think of nothin' but the warmth of his fingers. And how close he was. So close…but not close enough.

She scooted over a teeny bit, real casual-like, until their legs almost touched. Then she sighed, wonderin' if somebody'd turned up the radiator, or if this man was the one puttin' off all that sudden heat.

"Forget about it," he said softly. "You'd obviously never heard of what I did. But you figured it out…right quick."

The teasing smile on those lips of his told her he

was pokin' gentle fun. Not being mean. He was tryin' to talk on her level, to put her at ease. She liked him for that, she surely did.

"Drew?" she asked, nibbling her lip as she worked up her nerve to get the subject where she really wanted it. "Since I'm leavin' and all tomorrow, can I ask you a favor?"

"Don't leave tomorrow."

"I gotta…."

"No, you don't." He turned a little, facing her. "This is perfect for you, Tori. You're smart and you're quick and you're obviously bored with the life you've been living. You could improve your reading— I could help you."

Her eyes popped and she opened her mouth t'tell him he was crazier than a bedbug. But she couldn't. Because, dangit, the man was right. Wouldn't she love to get better at readin'. And she had been bored lately. Awful bored. Restless and wantin' somethin'…though she couldn't have said what.

Not until she stood right here in this very room earlier tonight. And set her eyes on all those books. All that learnin'.

Deep down, she hadn't been able to admit the truth, even in her own brain. A part of her had *wanted* to fulfill her promise to Daddy to get some education. Not mechanic'ing, not learnin' how to be all ladylike on a dumbass TV show, but *real* education. Ever since a few years ago when she started practicin' real hard to get better at readin'—good enough to pass her GED by the skin of her teeth—she'd wondered what it might be like to go back to school.

"I can see the hunger in you," Drew continued. He still had his hand on hers, and he started doing funny things with his fingers, runnin' 'em up and down softly, until her whole hand started to shake a bit. She wondered how fast he could make the rest of her body shake with that soft touch.

Probably faster than she could drive the quarter mile at Music City Raceway.

"Give yourself a chance to experience this, Tori. I think something special could happen for you here, in this house. It's just a few weeks out of your life."

My, but he sounded convincing. So reasonable, but strong. He nearly had her forgettin' how impossible it was. *Nearly.* She closed her eyes and grimaced as she pictured Luther's pretty, lazy little face all squished up and bruised. Sighing, she shook her head. "I cain't. I gotta get home and clean up a mess."

"I'm sure any mess in Sheets Creek will still be there in three weeks."

Yeah. She was pretty sure he was right. Knowin' Luther, there'd *always* be a mess.

He pushed her. "You know I'm right."

"You might be," she bit out, still looking at their hands, then at his khaki pants, so close to hers they overlapped onto her tight jeans.

"So you'll at least think about it?"

Unable to resist either the thought of learnin'…or the thought of *him* bein' the one teachin' her…she gave one short nod. "I'll think on it." Then she looked up at him and took a deep breath, for luck. "But in case I do get kicked outta here tomorrow, there's somethin' I gotta do, or I'll kick myself forever."

He waited, looking curious, apparently having no clue what she had in mind. Which made it that much easier to leap onto him and kiss the daylights outta the man.

She didn't give Drew a chance to say yes or no. She wanted a kiss from him, just one kiss to take with her, so she'd always remember at least once in her life she'd kissed a man who actually liked readin' more than the lotto numbers, the funny papers and the occasional verse outta the Good Book.

He gave one little grunt of surprise when she landed on his lap. Then he caught her in those big strong arms of his, pullin' her tight as their lips met.

Tori moaned a bit, she couldn't help it, he tasted *so* good. He had soft lips and sweet-tastin' breath. When she opened her mouth on his, he didn't get all sloppy and slobbery like every other man she'd ever kissed. No, his tongue met hers real gentlelike, as if he had to taste her, not swallow her whole.

He shifted a bit, keepin' her on his lap and droppin' one arm over her hip. Tori couldn't help feelin' every bump and bulge down there. Big bumps and bulges, truth be told.

That made her quiver even more.

"I've been wanting to do this since the moment I saw you," he said, real soft, against her lips.

She thought he meant kissin' her, which was what she'd been thinkin' about since the first second she set eyes on the man.

Then he showed her what he meant. He cupped her cheeks, kissin' her again; sweet, wet kisses, while slidin' his fingers into her hair. He wound it round his hands, playing with her curls.

Tori had never felt so...so...*cherished* was the only word her brain could think up. He treated her plain old hair as gentle and reverent as Tori treated her great grandma's antique linen tablecloth, the one she only took out at Christmas and Easter. Like it was precious and special.

He kissed her exactly the same way, sharin' breaths and soft nips and gentle thrusts of his tongue. Until she wanted to cry at how good she felt, down to the tips of her toes. Especially low in her belly. And lower, where she hadn't wanted any man to touch her in ages, not since she'd made the mistake of lettin' Billy Grayson do it to her in the back of his Camaro when she was twenty.

This wasn't nothin' like that. Billy'd been an overgrown kid, impatient and speedy on the trigger. Drew...oh, not only was he a man, he was a man who knew what to do to a woman. Because his kisses and his touches were sendin' her right outta her mind. She didn't expect this man would have to be apologizin' to a girl for it lastin' less time than it'd taken for Tori to unhook her bra.

When he stopped kissin' her, pullin' away so they could regain some distance, she wondered for a second if she was gonna die of disappointment. Oh, Lord-a-mercy did she wanna keep kissin' on and on and never stop.

A sucked in, shaky breath told her she was still among the livin'. Working up her nerve, she opened her eyes and found him starin' at her, a little smile on his lips, like someone who'd opened a pretty present.

"Thank you," he murmured.

"Welcome." Then, suckin' in a deep breath, she hopped off his lap. Shakin' her head in disappointment, she said what she knew was true. "Now I *gotta* go. That was a hello an' goodbye kiss. Just, you know, for my memory box."

"You have a memory box for kisses?"

She tapped the tip of her finger on her head. "In here. Where I keep all the special times tucked away."

He nodded, like he understood and had a memory box of his own. Before he could say anything, though, Tori figured the time had come for her to get away. Before she went and did somethin' even more stupid, like, oh, say, strippin' off her clothes and beggin' him to kiss her whole nekkid body the way he had her mouth.

"Bye, Drew. It was sure nice meetin' you. If you ever do decide to do some social studyin' down Tennessee way, look me up, okay?"

Then, not waiting for his answer, she dashed out of the room.

3

DREW WOKE UP VERY EARLY the next morning in the room he'd been assigned, after a long, restless night.

Tori. He'd thought of her through every waking moment, and she'd filled his dreams during what little sleep he'd managed.

Damn, but the woman got to him. And not just physically.

Yes, there had been an instant sexual attraction between them. She'd caught his eye at once and he'd been reacting to her on almost a primal level. After their kiss, that attraction had flared from a spark into a raging inferno.

But even more, he was attracted to her mind. To her wit. To the potential he saw in her. Because if there had ever been anyone ripe for learning and self-improvement, it was Tori Lyons. The enthusiasm in her voice and the innate sparkle in her eye told him so much about her. She not only needed it…she secretly *longed* for her life to change. He knew it like he knew his own ambitions, and he admired anyone who went after their dreams.

Well, usually. That philosophy had backfired on him at least once in the past, so Drew should know better than to even think of getting involved with someone with an uncertain future. He frowned as a less-pleasant memory surfaced. He hadn't thought of Sarah in a long time—months, at least—even though she'd once occupied his every waking thought.

Tori and Sarah were *nothing* alike, so his former fiancée shouldn't have intruded on his pleasant thoughts. Still, he supposed the woman he'd once planned to marry would never be completely erased from his mind. Not because he still cared for her, but because she'd made him look at every woman he met with a more jaundiced eye.

But not every woman was like her. Not even *most* women. And certainly not Tori. About the only thing they had in common was that they'd each faced real changes in their lives, the chance to reach for something more. Tori was about to reach for education.

Sarah had reached for money. Someone else's. She'd landed herself a rich plastic surgeon when she'd gone to Hollywood to pursue her dream of acting, putting her engagement to Drew on hold to do so.

"Forget her," he mumbled. Truthfully, he nearly had. Once she'd left, he knew it'd been for the best. He'd been practically a kid, just young and stupid, wanting what he thought he'd missed out on in his childhood—a real home, a family. Now, with his whirlwind life of world travel, well, he couldn't even fathom being settled down with a wife and kids somewhere.

That didn't mean he was immune to women. Especially not to Tori Lyons. Her unaffected charm and all her energy appealed to him, to the deepest part of Drew that few people really knew. They saw the college professor. The author. Not many people saw the wild kid who'd once had a similar sparkle and enthusiasm about everything in life. Or the man he became when he was away from the academic world, tromping through the jungle in South America or interacting with tribes in Africa.

That's probably what had appealed to him so much about Tori from the very beginning. She'd called to the part of him he kept so carefully contained in his daily life. The adventurer. The wanderer. The risk taker.

They were a lot alike, though she probably wouldn't believe it. He didn't let the world see the rough kid he'd once been. And she wouldn't let the world see the eager-for-knowledge woman lurking inside her, begging to be brought into the light.

He wanted to help her, encourage her, watch her become the incredible woman he sensed was beneath her rough exterior. Though he had to concede, she hadn't been rough all over.

Don't go there, he told himself, knowing he couldn't afford to think anymore of how soft and perfect she'd felt in his arms.

Tori might like to think she'd "stolen" a kiss for her memory box, but Drew knew better. He'd been surprised she'd made the first move—so very *forcefully*, which had delighted him—but she'd only done what *he'd* planned to do. He couldn't have gone back to his room last night without learning if she tasted as sweet as she looked, if she felt as delightful as she sounded.

She had. She'd surpassed every expectation, until he felt like he was stumbling into something new and rare. Then she'd left. He'd had to watch her walk away when all he wanted was to pull her back down and let her feel what she'd done to him.

His groin tightened. Again. Just at the thought.

Calling himself an ass, he got out of bed and

headed for the bathroom adjoining his suite. A cold shower. That's what he needed. *Or her warm body.*

No. It couldn't happen. He'd been strong enough to let her go last night, when he knew, with a few words, they could both have been naked and panting on that couch.

One thing had stopped him. No matter what Burt Mueller and his crew said about the show not kicking off officially until today, he wouldn't put it past the man to have had cameras already up and running last night.

Bad enough to be caught kissing one of the women he was supposed to be helping the very first night. If he'd made love to her, he'd have humiliated her completely. And ruined any chance he had of getting her to stay—for the *right* reasons.

After his shower he dressed quickly, then left his room to seek out Mr. Mueller. They had some talking to do. He was going to stay here and see this thing through, but only on one condition. That his number-one pupil stay, also.

If Tori went, so did he.

Which was *exactly* what he told Burt Mueller when he tracked him down in the enormous dining room. The producer was talking with the director, a man named Niles Monahan, whom Drew had met last night. Monahan was a quiet, nervous type, who barely said a word when the effusive producer was around. He quickly made himself scarce, apparently hearing the curtness in Drew's tone.

Just as well. Monahan had no power. Mueller planned to leave today or tomorrow, but he'd most certainly call the shots in this production, even if from a distance.

"Tori Lyons..." Mueller said, his brow pulling down in concentration.

"The race-car driver," someone murmured.

Drew glanced at the lead camera operator, who'd been introduced as Jacey Turner the evening before. A slim, pale-skinned brunette dressed all in black, the woman had huge brown eyes that dominated her face. And she always seemed aware of everything that was happening around her. A listener, that one. She'd be the one who'd expose any and all secrets taking place in this house over the next few weeks. No doubt about it.

Now she was standing on a chair, setting up a camera shot over the expansive dining room table, apparently listening to every word they said.

"Exactly. She has the potential to really make this work," Drew explained, striving to remain detached and not let them see how much he, personally, wanted Tori to remain.

"You know this after a short glimpse of the women yesterday afternoon?" Mueller asked, his stare pointed.

Drew managed an even nod.

"Or because of your conversation in the library last night?" Jacey's voice was deceptively light.

"Sonofabitch," Drew muttered.

"Ahh, ahh," Mueller said with an all-too-innocent smile. "You knew the house was wired."

"You said the cameras were off until today."

The man simply shrugged. His camera operator gave Drew a sympathetic look. "Everyone associated with the show signed a release stating they knew they might be filmed any time from the minute they arrived." She paused. "Including you."

"I see. So it was my error for actually *believing* what you said." Drew gave a humorless laugh. "I forgot the type of people I was dealing with. A mistake I won't make again."

Jacey's eyes widened. She and Burt exchanged a quick glance, a look Drew recognized. Same old story. People saw the credentials or his polite manner and assumed he was some kind of damn pushover.

They had a lot to learn. A whole lot.

"As I recall," Drew added, remaining calm in spite of his inner fury, "I stipulated in the contract we both signed that I would be taped in any common areas of the house, but *not* in my private quarters." He stared at Mueller, hard, until the man's eyes shifted away and his face flushed. The pink color crept all the way up his forehead onto his bald pate.

"I'll be returning to my room in one hour," Drew bit out. "If there are any cameras in it, I will consider you in violation of our written contract. I will leave these premises immediately and will be calling my attorney."

Then he looked at Jacey, who continued to watch, wide-eyed.

"I know what you're thinking, Miss Turner. That you're rather adept at hiding small electronic devices." Her eyes flared a bit, but she kept still. She was better at this than her boss, he had to give her that much.

With a tight smile, he added, "But believe me, if I can find a shard of three-thousand-year-old pottery buried in the side of a South American mountain, I can surely find any type of camera or microphone you've planted in my room."

Drew didn't bother adding that when he was twelve, he, his mother and his sister had lived for weeks in a basement storage room of a shopping mall. He'd become quite familiar with electronic security equipment. How to spot it. How to avoid it. How to disable it.

He sensed they wouldn't believe him, anyway.

He turned his attention back to Mueller. "I trust I'm making myself clear?"

The man nodded once, obviously not liking being bested.

Well, neither did Drew. Not in anything.

He turned to leave the dining room, but before exiting completely, he said over his shoulder, "And by the way, about Miss Lyons? I mean it. She's the best shot you've got at making this thing work. You'd better hold on to her, no matter what it takes."

He didn't even turn around, or wait for a reaction. As he strode out of the room, he heard Jacey Turner mumble to her boss, "I think we might have underestimated him."

Stalking down the hall toward the front door, where he planned to get in his car and drive off his rage for an hour while they cleared his room of bugs, he nodded in agreement.

Yeah. They had underestimated him.

But they wouldn't again.

TORI WOKE UP, AS USUAL, with the sun. Her roommate, Sukie—thank the Lord she'd ended up with *her* and not Ginny the flasher or one of the other wild girls— was still sawin' logs, even though it was nigh on seven in the mornin'.

Tori hated to slug-a-bed. So real quiet, she got up and gathered her clothes. She knew the cameras went on today and didn't trust the TV people not to have the little spy doohickeys every which place. So she planned to do *all* her undressin' in the bathroom. They'd put that much in writin'—no bathroom stuff. Guaranteed.

If she stayed around, she'd probably spend a fair amount of time in here. The big tub looked nice and comfy... She sure could do some readin' in it. But, she reminded herself, she *wasn't* staying around.

She'd kept her promise to Drew and thought on it all night. She just couldn't come up with any way around it. She had to bail her brother outta his troubles, no matter how much she wanted to stay. Which, to her genuine amazement, she *did*.

Sukie still wasn't up by the time she came back out, but Tori was ready to start her day, anyway. So she left her room, countin' doors down the hall, tryin' to remember how to get back to her own. Hopefully, she'd be comin' back soon to pack up and go home.

"It's for the best," she whispered, thinkin' about Luther and his problem. But boy, it sure did hurt for some reason. Part of her got all tight and achy when she thought about leavin'.

The horny part.

She shushed the little voice in her brain. Because yeah, she sure wouldn't mind spendin' some more time with Drew Bennett...between the sheets. Or on the sofa. Or the big fancy piano, or the dinin' room table or any old place.

But there was more than that. She'd liked him. Dangitall, why'd she have to go and meet a man who made her all shivery inside, and also made her mind start doin' leapfrogs with all the ideas he put in her head? Like about her readin' better. Learnin' about places, and...*societies*...like he did.

She didn't just want to learn from him. She liked talkin' to him. Liked listenin' to him. Lookin' at him get all energetic when he'd tried to sweet-talk her into stayin'.

He made her want—*more*. To sound like him. To think like him.

To get nekkid with him, girl, that's all this is about, so forget about it right now!

She wasn't about to start arguin' with the voice in her head. Because it usually won.

Needing some alone time before breakfast, Tori bee-lined for the front door. They couldn't have wired the whole yard with cameras. Leastwise, she hoped not!

She grabbed her heavy coat from the front closet and tugged it on over her sweater, fastening it up tight. Good thing, because when she stepped out-side, the cold mornin' air made her breaths turn to icicles in her lungs. It stung a bit. But a good kinda sting…the kind that reminded a body it was still alive and kickin'.

Shoving her hands into her pockets, she curled her fingers tight. Too bad she hadn't thought to buy some gloves during the overnight stay in Albany. "No matter," she told herself. "You'll be home before you woulda been able to get any use out of 'em."

Somebody'd done a good job shovelin' all the snow off the front walk, but Tori was mindful of overnight ice as she walked down it. Then she mulled it over, re-alizin', suddenly, that she'd known all along where she wanted to go. She didn't have the right shoes on for a tromp through the snow, but she figured her work boots were at least a little bit waterproof.

Veering off the walk, she headed for the building she'd spied yesterday on the way in. It was a strange-lookin' thing—all glass walls, shiny and sparkly in the sunlight. She'd seen the reflection of it this mornin' from her bedroom window, which had gotten her curiosity all riled up again.

As she got closer, she realized what it was. "A greenhouse," she whispered, her breath making misty clouds in front've her face. She never knowed people had such things in their own yards, and had only ever seen them on TV commercials for plant nurseries.

This one was glassy and huge, steamy water coverin' the walls, probably from whatever plants were growin' inside. She wanted to see them. Wanted to see green plants and springtime in this place that was covered with a pretty—but lifeless—blanket of snow.

Tori had a green thumb. Some of her earliest memories were of pullin' weeds with her mama in their vegetable garden. On days when she needed to be alone—away from family and the track and the feelin' she was missin' something—she liked nothing better than to spend hours in the garden. She'd kneel down in the dirt, her fingers in the earth as she coaxed the little sprouts of peas or green beans, and she'd forget her troubles for awhile.

"Wonder if they got weeds in greenhouses?" she muttered, thinkin' she had a lotta troubles she'd like to forget this mornin'.

It was worth a look-see.

Opening the door, she stepped in almost sideways, keepin' her back to the inside and her face to the wall. She wanted to see everything all at once, not just bits and pieces as she came in. So after carefully pushin' the door shut, she clamped her eyes closed. She kept them that way as she swiveled on her heel to face the room.

Her skin reacted right away to the difference in the inside air, so odd after bein' outside. It felt thick and wet, heavy as it went down her windpipe. And *hot*. But it also smelled so sweet, of earth and flowers, that she couldn't help just standin' there, suckin' it in for a spell.

Finally, when she was almost light-headed with the deep breaths of earthy air, she opened her eyes.

And froze.

"Jeezum crow," she whispered.

Her jaw dropped open as she stared around in wonder, feelin' like a little kid lookin' at pretty wrappin's on a roomful'a Christmas presents. All ablaze with lights and colors and shiny, glittery decorations.

Lordy, she'd never seen a prettier sight. Huge clumps of green plants filled the place. Row after row of palmy lookin' things, graceful and slim, almost bowin' to each other under a soft breeze comin' from an overhead fan.

And the flowers... "Oh, mercy," she whispered, entranced by the brilliant hues. Red and orange and a yellow so pure it looked like the petals had been dipped in sunshine.

Nothin' simple like daisies or roses, these flowers were all jaggedy and strange but still perfect. Bloomin' in exotic shapes and points, but so darn lovely, they took her breath away.

"My, oh, my, it's like God's own garden," she whispered.

"It is, isn't it?"

Almost leaping, she blinked and peered around the corner of a big old plant with spiky-lookin' orange flowers that almost looked like birds' heads. Her heart tripped over itself, flutterin' all inside her chest, when she saw who'd spoken. "It's you."

"We've got to stop meeting like this," Drew said with a wide smile.

"Let's don't."

He chuckled. "I see I wasn't the only one who got an early start today."

"I can't stay abed once the sun's in the sky," she replied, wonderin' if fate had brought her out here this mornin' so she could see him one more time before she left.

Drew stepped out from behind the plant, until he stood next to her. He'd taken off his jacket, it was so warm in here, and had it slung over his shoulder. A tiny bit of moisture—sweat, or humidity—shone on the sunken-in part of his throat. Tori suddenly had the strangest feelin'. Her mouth went dry, wonderin' how that little spot of wetness would taste if she leaned over and licked it right off of his skin. Salty, she'd bet. Salty and sweet and absolutely delicious.

She finally got her attention off the shiny skin and forced herself to look around the greenhouse. Unfortunately, the flowers weren't near as nice to look at.

"I never seen so many beautiful plants," Tori said.

Drew stared around, too, and nodded. "I haven't, either." Then he turned his attention solely to her. "Why are you out here? Shouldn't you be getting ready for breakfast?"

"I could ask you the same question."

He shrugged. "I wasn't invited."

"That ain't very polite."

"I don't mind. The director wants to talk to all of you. I'm not an active part of the show."

Feeling much warmer herself now, Tori slipped

her coat off her back and draped it over a tall pile of unused planter boxes. "What is your part on the show, anyway?"

Drew's coat joined hers. He was again wearing what he probably thought was casual, comfortable clothes. Back home, comfortable and casual meant jeans. She'd like to see this man in a pair of sinful tight jeans. But these dressy pants, loose where they needed to be but right snug across the front—where it *really* counted—were nice, too.

"I'm not entirely sure. I'm supposed to be some kind of overseer. To gauge everyone's progress and help where I can."

"You're not, like, the celebrity host or something?"

"Good God, no," he said with a shudder. "I didn't want any active part in this at all, but allowed myself to be convinced. Believe me, I *hate* having any part of my personal life exposed on television for public consumption. I value my privacy and intend to stay as far out of camera range as possible." Then he gave her a serious look. "Tell me you're staying."

She sucked her lip into her mouth, hatin' to disappoint him. And knowin' he would be disappointed, though they hadn't known each other but for one day. "Sorry," she mumbled. "I can't."

His face went frowny. "You said you'd think about it."

"I did. All night." A yawn came over her then, just to prove the point.

He smiled. "I didn't sleep well, either."

"Was it them snails?"

Shaking his head, he stepped a bit closer. "No, it was our kiss."

Oh. *That.* "Well, uh, that was one'a them…instinctual things," she mumbled.

"See a man, kiss him?" His voice held an edge.

She slowly shook her head. "Huh-uh. See a dead-sexy man, talk to him a spell and find out he's got brains to go with the looks and a smile to make you forget all your troubles. Figure you ain't never gonna see him again so you better take your shot." She shrugged. "*Then* kiss him."

He nodded, lookin' like he was thinkin' things over, before coming even closer. "Funny," he said, real softlike, "but you telling me you're leaving has suddenly aroused the same instinctual reaction in me."

But before Tori could figure out what he meant, he put his arms around her and pulled her close.

Then he showed her.

DREW HADN'T INTENDED to kiss Tori. But the thought of her leaving—of never seeing her again—got to him. Especially because of her explanation about why she'd kissed him…because she'd sensed there was something special between them and it was never going to be explored.

He felt the same way. She was beautiful. Funny. Smart. Had an irresistible smile.

And was leaving.

That, more than anything, made him pull her into his arms and press a hot, languorous kiss on her lips. She parted them immediately, licking at him, sucking his tongue into her mouth. Curling against his body, she moaned a little. Or maybe he did. He couldn't be sure.

Kissing her suddenly didn't seem enough. He wanted to feel her smooth skin beneath his fingers.

Unable to resist, he slid his hands to her waist, easily moving under the bottom hem of her sweater, and lightly stroked her bare skin.

Just as soft, supple and appealing.

He groaned, allowing Tori to pull him even tighter against her, until not a sliver of humid air could come between them. The place was steaming hot and rapidly becoming more so. All he wanted was to take off his clothes—and hers—and make love to her right here in this heady-smelling place.

Reason reared its ugly head. *You can't do this.*

He slowly—ruefully—ended their kiss and stepped back. Then he looked around, wondering just how desperate Burt Mueller was. Would he really risk expensive camera equipment by outfitting this greenhouse? Doubtful. There wasn't one corner of the room that wouldn't get misty. Besides, there were no unexposed hidden spots to conceal a camera.

So *this* kiss, at least, should remain private.

"Wow…you can say goodbye to me anytime you want," she whispered, sounding a little dazed.

He slowly backed away, trying to regain control of his brain and his impulses. "I don't want to. Tell me why you have to leave."

And suddenly, to his great surprise, she did. He listened to her explanation, eyes widening in disbelief. When she'd finished, his jaw stiffened and he frowned. "So you're telling me you're going to give up something I know damn well you want…" Her eyes flared, but she didn't deny his words. "So you can go bail out your spoiled brother who needs to grow up and learn to solve his own problems?"

"When you put it that way, it don't sound too smart."

"What's the matter with letting your father—Luther's *parent*—help him get himself out of this mess?"

Seeing the quivering of Tori's beautiful lips, he suspected what she'd say. She *felt* like a parent, though, if he remembered the yearly sequence right, she was only two years older than Luther.

"Never mind. I understand," he muttered. And he meant it. Sweeping a frustrated hand through his hair, he explained, "I have a sister who's three years younger than me, and I started feeling responsible for her by the time she was old enough to walk. Still do, really."

There could have been a long explanation. Anyone else might have asked a million questions. About whether he'd had a father around. If he'd had a normal childhood. Why a little boy would feel responsible for his baby sister's welfare.

Tori didn't ask a thing. She simply…got it. A slight nod told him she completely understood. Because she'd been there herself.

"Don't leave, Tori," he found himself saying, his voice low and intense. "You can't return to your old life and step back into that role because you'll never break out of it if you don't take your shot now." Trying to lighten his tone, he continued. "This is just a silly show on the outside. But it's a start. I'll work with you on your reading, and you'll have other teachers with you day and night. You can come out of this ready to tackle any kind of future you envision for yourself."

She met his stare, her blue eyes shining. With the moisture from the air? Or her unshed tears? He couldn't tell. But sensing he had the advantage, he reached out and touched her hair, brushing it off her face until he had her full attention.

"If you leave you'll regret it for the rest of your life."

Thinking of the similar choice he'd been forced to make—when his aunt and uncle had taken him and his sister into their home, demanding nothing more for their love than that he give everything he had into turning his life around—he knew he was right.

Finally, after a long, silent moment filled with expectation and uncertainty, she offered him a tentative smile.

"I'll stay."

BREAKFAST WAS a whole lot quieter than dinner had been the night before. Tori figured all the girls were on their best behavior, mindful of the cameras and crew. Not to mention the frowny-faced, sniffly little director guy.

She'd made it back from the greenhouse just as the rest of the girls came downstairs. Nobody seemed to have missed her, thank the Lord. Drew hadn't come in with her, sayin' he figured it'd be best for them not to come back together. She didn't see what difference it made, but figured somebody might accuse him of givin' her extra help.

He'd been givin' her *somethin'* in the greenhouse, but that was nobody else's business.

They tried to feed 'em some fancy breakfast food, but Tori wasn't havin' any part of that smoked fish stuff and stuck to the fruit and rolls. While she nibbled it, she looked around the room at the other fifteen girls, wonderin' which of them would be gone by tomorrow mornin'.

"You decided not to pick your nose?" someone whispered in her right ear.

She looked over and saw Sukie smilin' her big smile and crackin' her gum between her teeth.

"I think I'll stick it out for a spell."

"Good," Sukie said. "'Cause I don't want anybody else for a roommate." She looked around the table at the other women and lowered her voice even more. "Ginny said Robin was snoring all night, loud enough to wake the dead."

Tori snickered. "Ginny shoulda just pulled her knockers on either side'a her head to block out the noise."

Sukie snorted and barked a laugh. A couple of girls glanced over, and Tori shoved a piece of banana into her mouth, suddenly feeling a little bad. Good thing they'd been whisperin'—nobody else could hear them.

She didn't like catty women and didn't consider herself one of 'em. Bein' around men all the time, she was glad for the chance to talk to *any* livin' female. That'd be another bright part of stickin' around this place. There were lotsa females to make friends with.

Deciding to watch her sassy mouth from now on, she glanced around and met the eye of the dark-haired camerawoman. She was laughin' beneath her breath, and when her stare met Tori's, her eyes twinkled. The other woman's grin told Tori she'd been overheard.

Dang them microphones.

"Ladies, may I have your attention, please?"

The producer, Mr. Mueller, tapped his spoon on the side of his glass to get their attention. Tori put down her fork and looked at him. So did everyone else.

Mueller looked just exactly what she'd expect a Hollywood type to look like. Fancy suit with a bit of a shine in the material. Smooth face that'd been under the knife once or twice. Big ole white teeth.

Bald and shiny head, kinda big for his shoulders. Yep. He somehow fit the Hollywood she'd always imagined.

"As you know," he was sayin', "you're all about to undergo an intensive crash course in…socialization." He smiled his big white smile. "We will be breaking you up into smaller groups and rotating you through lessons throughout the day, as outlined in the information packet you received weeks ago."

Yeah. Tori remembered. Classes from everything on how to talk good, to which fork to use at dinner. Even how to walk.

She couldn't care less about that. But she did look forward to the grammar and real book-learnin'. Not just because she really wanted to learn those things, but because Drew would most likely be the one teachin' them.

"What you *don't* know," Mr. Mueller said, "is that we have another agenda. A secret agenda, for all of you. One that could make someone in this room very, very wealthy."

The girls all sat up straight, ears open as big as their eyes now.

Mueller shared a look with the camerawoman in black. Then he turned his attention back to them. "You see, we've decided to truly up the stakes in this transformation game. Now, you're not only competing for a chance to attend a society gala in New York during the holidays, as well as the wardrobe and jewelry for the trip." He paused, and all the girls around the table almost held their breath, waitin' to hear what the man was getting at. "One of you ladies might leave this place at the end of the month with a cool million dollars."

Tori's jaw dropped. Sukie muttered a swear word. Ginny whooped. A few others started askin' questions and gigglin'.

Mueller gave them all a couple of seconds to mull it over, then he held up his hand, askin' for their attention again. "I know you're all curious about what might be required of you. In fact, it's very simple." He pointed to a big screen hangin' on the wall just behind him. Nothin' was showing yet, but one of his tech guys was fiddlin' with a computer.

While they waited for the picture to flash up there, Mueller looked around the room, nodding to himself. Then, actin' all calm and quiet in spite of the twinkle in his eye and the way he almost was bouncing in excitement, he dropped the bomb. "All you have to do to win the million dollars," he said with a broad smile, "is get someone to fall in love with you."

A bunch of whispers started again, while the computer guy flicked a switch and a big giant computer page appeared on the overhead screen.

"It might sound unusual, but if you look at the target you will certainly agree it shouldn't be a hardship," Mueller said softly, pointin' to the image.

Everyone froze, watching a picture appear.

Tori felt a flutterin' in her stomach. She didn't have the second sight, like her cousin Peachy, who'd been born with a caul over her face. Still, sometimes she had a little shine. Intuition or somethin'.

Right now, hers was screamin' that she knew whose face she was gonna see any second.

"Ladies," Mr. Mueller said, "here is your objective. To win the money, get the man pictured right there to tell you he loves you, before the lady of them all is announced on December twenty-second."

Tori scrunched her eyes shut, not wantin' to see. Around her, the girls all started jabberin' and oohin' and aahin'.

Finally, she took a deep breath and slowly opened her eyes. And saw his face. His dark-as-pitch hair, those shiny eyes. That dent in his cheek from his big ole smile.

She wanted to cry. Because for the next two-and-a-half weeks, every woman in this place was gonna be competin' for *him*.

Drew Bennett.

4

To Drew's great disappointment, he didn't see Tori much at all the first few days of taping. He told himself it was only because of her busy schedule, but had to wonder if she was avoiding him. If their unexpected attraction to each other had scared her off, instead of intriguing her, as it had him.

Still, he had to give thanks for small favors: she hadn't left.

On the first night, the sixteen women had been reduced in number to twelve. The four least-promising subjects had been whisked out of the mansion, under guard, not exchanging a word with anyone. Drew hadn't been part of the team doing the choosing, to his surprise, and he'd had a few tense moments worrying about Tori. But she'd been fine.

Late that night, he'd mulled over the four names, wondering if Mueller had intentionally eliminated the four least attractive of the women, or if Drew was being jaded about Hollywood these days. As if there was any time it *wasn't* okay to be jaded about Hollywood.

The following morning, the dozen had been divided into four groups of three and each group had begun a rigorous schedule of training. Drew, himself, taught a current events class designed to aid the women with conversation in social settings. But Tori hadn't shown up with her group. Not yesterday or today. Though she'd claimed to be sick, Drew had questioned that. Because she hadn't missed any of her *other* classes.

Mueller had brought in several instructors—including a former English teacher, a dance instructor, a hair, makeup and wardrobe professional, a maître d'. Even a woman who wrote a column called "Auntie Etiquette" for a New England paper. And Tori had been right there working with every one of them, looking earnest and intent every time he'd walked by an open door and seen her. But she'd blown *him* off. Which was really unsettling.

Even worse than not wanting to see him with her group, she hadn't made any effort to seek him out alone.

Unlike just about every other woman on the set.

"Come on, Professor, don't ya want to see what you've got to work with?" asked a blonde named Teresa. Teresa, who'd seemed more interested in Hollywood gossip than current events during his class, was the woman he'd dubbed the pole dancer the day of his arrival.

"Thank you, but no," Drew murmured, wondering how she'd managed to trap him, alone, in the sunroom, when he'd taken such pains to avoid letting anyone see him enter. It seemed wherever he went in this place, one of the women always managed to find him. He could accept it from the crew, who kept track of everyone with their cameras. But the female contestants on the set seemed to have built-in radar to his location every minute of the day.

Drew had never lacked for female company whenever he desired it. And sometimes when he didn't. He'd certainly been on the receiving end of a lot of come-ons from his students over the years, and he'd heard a lot of Indiana Jones comments. The women in this house, however, were acting like a nuclear holocaust had taken place and he was the last male on the planet.

Which needed rapid repopulating.

"You know you wanna see what I got," Teresa said as she reached up and ran her fingertips across his cheek.

"No, I really don't."

She chuckled, running her hand down his neck. He leaned back, his body language doing the talking.

She didn't listen to that, either. "Watch, now, I'm gonna give you the kind of private show guys usually pay a hundred bucks for."

Drew frowned. "I'm sure your dance instructor will be happy to review your skills before he begins teaching you…uh…" *Something other than a bump and grind.* "Ballroom dancing."

"*Watch,*" she said, obviously not taking *no* for an answer. Since she stood between Drew and the only exit, he didn't have much choice.

Teresa began to hum a low, thrumming tune, and started to gyrate like a she-wolf in heat. He supposed the expression on her face—eyes half-closed, lips pursed—was meant to represent orgasmic ecstasy. Instead she merely looked like she'd eaten something unpleasant.

"Teresa, I really have to go. And so do you. You're late for something, I'm sure."

"Wait, it hasn't even started getting good!"

She reached for a floor lamp.

Okay, that's it. Time to make his exit.

"Ooh, baby, yeah," she moaned, licking her lips.

Men actually paid money to see this? He began to feel sorry for the owners of this house, who'd rented their place to Mueller for the month. They were going to have to pay someone to come in and disinfect all of their lamps. At least the ones in the rooms Teresa had inhabited.

"Oooh, you know you love it," she was saying through heavy breaths as she did mildly obscene things to the poor brass light-fixture.

"Nice," he muttered.

She obviously didn't hear his sarcasm. "I'm just gettin' started." Still holding the lamp with one hand, she lifted her other to unzip her dress.

"Whoa," Drew said, wondering if Burt Mueller was spiking the women's food with some kind of aphrodisiac. "Sorry, but I'm not interested in…uh… any more of your dancing."

While her hands were occupied, he moved smoothly around her and out the door.

"Hey, Professor, wait," she called. "It's just getting good."

Hearing a crash, he cringed over the loss of the lamp. The poor thing had probably thrown itself to its death to get out from between Teresa's well-used thighs.

Ducking down a hallway, which would put him out of sight-range of Teresa when she exited the sunroom, he paused to get his bearings. The house was huge. But it wasn't big enough to give him any privacy whatsoever. The only time he'd been alone since yesterday morning was when he was firmly ensconced in his room. And considering the way four of the women had felt free to stroll right in, he'd had to start locking the door!

"This is crazy," he muttered aloud.

Very crazy. The whole thing. He was supposed to be overseeing some lessons. Not having to hide from a bunch of amorous women who wanted to get a little extracurricular with the teacher.

His frustration was made worse because he'd been unable to see the only person in this asylum whom he really *wanted* to see. Tori.

Glancing at his watch, he noted it was nearly four. He'd checked the posted schedule this morning and knew Tori's group was, at this time, supposed to be in the kitchen getting lessons in food appreciation and table manners.

Hopefully that would prevent any more food fights, like the one this afternoon at lunch. Drew had been dining with Group B, and had made the mistake of complimenting one of the women—a very tall redhead named Robin—on her knowledge of cutlery.

Robin had ended up with a face full of cold soup, courtesy of Ginny. Then it'd turned into a free-for-all. Even after grabbing a quick, midday shower, Drew still smelled the lingering, cloying sweetness of keylime pie in his hair.

Pie. The kitchen. Tori.

He didn't hesitate and began striding down the hallway, determined to see her and find out why she'd been avoiding him.

Another of the contestants, however, had other ideas.

"Hey there, Professor," a tawny-skinned woman said as she stepped out from an inset doorway. It almost felt as if she'd been lying in wait for him.

"Aren't you supposed to be in your speech class?" Drew asked absently, trying not to slow down.

She planted herself right in front of him. "I'm already very good at speaking," she said, licking her lips. "Come here and I'll whisper something special in your ear." She smiled, her sharp teeth white and glistening.

He'd sooner put his ear next to an open flame.

"Uh, Simone, I'm not even scheduled to conduct the first evaluation until Friday. There's really no need for you to display your...skills." He shook his head, seizing on what seemed to be the only logical explanation. "All of you seem to be under the mistaken impression that currying my favor is going to aid you in some way."

"It's not your favor I'm after," she said, putting her hand flat on his chest and batting her heavily made-up eyes.

"I'm your teacher," he snapped.

"I can teach you a few things."

"*Goddamn* it," he muttered, suddenly having enough of this, "have you all completely lost it?"

Simone pouted, obviously not realizing she'd pushed him too far. "Chill babe, let me help you work off some of that frustration."

"Look," he said, trying to maintain his calm, "you're here to learn. To gain some polish, some social skills. Not to get laid."

"How do you know?" she countered.

Drew merely gritted his teeth, gave her the kind of withering stare that had intimidated every obnoxious student he'd ever had, then strode past her.

He wished he could confront Mueller, but it was too late. The man had left, whirling onto his next big project, leaving the soft-voiced director, Niles Monahan, in charge. And Monahan had about as much chance of getting a dozen horny women to behave as Drew had of sprouting wings and flying out of this madhouse.

Shaking his head, he drew in a few deep breaths, trying to regain his calm, rational mood. It'd somehow deserted him in the past few days.

He should go to his room or his car—the two places where he could lock himself in, away from the cameras and the women.

But he didn't. He headed straight for the kitchen.

TORI HAD BEEN TRYIN'—try*ing*—to figure out how to handle things ever since Mr. Mueller had dropped his bomb Sunday at breakfast. She'd fumed about it and even, to her mortification, cried about it, but couldn't figure a way around the truth.

Drew was the stakes and a million smackers was the prize.

Her first instinct had been to leave. She'd tell the director she'd changed her mind and skedaddle on home. Because this silly competition stuff just made her feel…nasty.

Drew Bennett would *hate* bein' some kinda prey for the women on this here show. *Being* she reminded herself, mindful of the way the snippy-faced English teacher had made Tori repeat the phrase *ing* about a half a gajillion times over the past few days.

For sure, Drew would blow a gasket when this romance competition came to light. He'd said as much before, telling her he planned to stay out of camera sight as much as possible, to keep his private life private.

She was tempted to tell him herself, only, the contract she'd signed might get her into trouble if she did. She remembered a buncha legal mumbo jumbo in there, but one thing stuck out—if any part of the so-called secrecy agreement got violated, she had to pay back every penny they'd put into her, including her airfare, her food, her education expenses and who knew what all.

Her next instinct had been to break her promise and get herself kicked out. Because she liked him too much to stay and watch what these greedy, horny women were gonna do to him.

But she *wanted* him too much to leave and let them do it!

There was no denying it, she wanted him for herself. Not because of any cash prize—because, while she knew for sure he was interested in her, she didn't for one second believe a handsome, wealthy college professor was gonna go prostrating himself with love for *her*.

No, money didn't factor into it. *He* did. It was all about Drew Bennett. His smile and his laugh and his brains. Not to mention the way he'd made her feel from the first minute she'd set eyes on him: hungry and empty and wanting and needy.

And very special.

"Special," she whispered under her breath, feeling a little shivery when she said it.

Because he had. From the first word he'd said, the first look he'd given her, he'd made her see herself differently. Not as rough-edged Tori who'd beat up a man soon's look at him. But as a pretty woman with a brain and a real chance to do something with her life.

Why, oh *why*, had Mueller gone and ruined things by turning this simple makeover show into a manhunt? She might actually be enjoying herself if he hadn't gone and changed the rules. Though it'd been hard work, she really liked the stuff she was learning from the English teacher. She was even beginning to correct herself in her own thoughts, which oughta count for something.

But ever since the real point of this show had been announced, she seemed to be the *only* one interested in learning a darn thing.

"I don't get why we still have to do this stuff like knowing whether to drink white wine or red with dinner, now that we know what the real object of this game is," said Tiffany, a young blond girl from California. Tiffany had more hair than brains. And less clothes than Britney Spears.

Tori coulda told her Drew Bennett would never fall in love with someone who wouldn't even try to use the smarts God'd given her. She wasn't, however, that charitable. Let the wolves figure it out themselves; she planned to stay right out of it.

Only, she couldn't, could she? Her mind might not want to do something as low-down dirty and rotten as compete for the man for money. But her body wanted him. Wanted him bad.

Which was why she'd done her best to just steer clear of the man. Leastwise until she could figure out what to do.

"Well, what I don't get is why you can't always drink pink wine no matter what you're eating, and forget about it," Sukie muttered, glaring at the glasses spread out in front of them on the big butcher-block kitchen counter.

Tori was with Sukie. Made sense to her.

"Because," a smooth male voice said, "if you order

the wrong wine at *some* restaurants, you'll end up getting lousy service from a snotty waiter who thinks he's smarter than you."

Tori's—everyone's—gaze shot to the doorway, where a smiling Drew Bennett watched them.

Oh, my, he looked good to her. His dark hair gleamed and his sexy smile made her shake right in her boots. And made dollar signs light up in the minds of every other woman in the room.

Shoot me now.

"Oooh," Tiffany said, practically cooing as she stuck her lips out. Not to mention her chest. "I never thought of it that way. Maybe we could go to a nice restaurant sometime to get something…" she licked her lips and lowered her voice, "to *eat.*"

Tori rolled her eyes. Was there anything more nauseating than a blond bimbo trying out tricks on another woman's man?

Whoa, there, girl. He ain't yours.

No. He wasn't hers. She might want him to be, but he was fair game. Literally, thanks to Mr. Mueller, who'd made him the birdie and this here duck season.

"I'm sure you'll have lots of chances to practice right here, Miss Myers," he said to Tiffany, his voice all cool and even. Tori hadn't heard that tone before. It didn't sound nothing…*anything*…like the way he talked when they were alone.

"Professor?" Sukie straightened in her seat and tapped her finger on the countertop, waiting for his attention.

He turned toward her. "Yes, Miss Green?"

"Well, I wanted you to know that I've been thinking all afternoon about the little problem in the Middle East that we're supposed to talk about in class tomorrow."

Little problem? If that place had a little problem, Tori figured World War II musta been a friendly spat.

"Oh?" Drew said, sounding a bit more polite and interested as he gave Sukie his full attention.

"Uh-huh. I think the answer is to make them all become Scientologists."

Tiffany snorted, sounding just like the pet hog Tori'd had when she was a kid. "How many hairdressers do you think one country needs, especially since the women all have to wear those veils?"

Hairdressers. Tori rolled her eyes, thinking Tiffany had got whacked with a stupid stick one too many times in her life.

Sukie glared. "It's a religion, you…you…blonde!" Then she looked at Drew. "Then they wouldn't have anything to fight over. And John Travolta could go visit them and teach them to dance, because people who dance together don't usually want to kill each other afterward. Especially with as good a dancer as John Travolta."

Tori lowered her head so Sukie wouldn't see her laugh. She liked Sukie a lot, but dang, sometimes the girl didn't make a lick of sense.

Drew kept a straight face. "Interesting idea. Maybe we can talk it out as a group tomorrow."

Then he cleared his throat.

Tori didn't look up. She knew he was staring at her, heck, she practically felt the burning of his eyes on her face. But she couldn't meet that stare, not without flinching and blushing and letting him and the whole TV world see every thought going on inside her head.

"Tori," he said, stepping closer.

She could see the tips of his brown shoes beside the feet of her stool and felt the brush of his hip against her side.

Lord gimme strength.

"I heard you were sick earlier," he said. "Are you feeling okay now?"

She nodded. "I'm fine."

"Good. Then maybe you can give me some time so I can catch you up with the rest of your group."

She peeked up. He didn't even give her a chance to answer, he just looked at the woman teaching the class—who was watching him all wide-eyed with interest, even though she didn't have a million-dollar bone being dangled in front of her face. The man probably caused that reaction in every woman he met. He sure was handsome enough to.

"I'm sure you won't mind if Tori cuts out of this lesson a few minutes early. I think I can catch her up before dinner."

Tori gulped, very aware of the stares of the other contestants. Not to mention the one of the dark-haired camerawoman, Jacey, who seemed to follow Tori around everywhere these days. "I don't mind...."

He didn't give her time to argue. Or give the kitchen lady time to answer. He just took her by the arm and practically hoisted her off her stool.

Which was when she figured out he was mad. Darn mad. At her.

"WHY HAVE YOU BEEN avoiding me?"

Drew frankly didn't care about the cameras or anyone who might be watching as he practically hauled Tori out of the kitchen, toward the front stairs.

"I dunno what you mean."

"Like hell you don't."

When she almost stumbled, he slowed down. But his steps remained deliberate. "Why?"

"I ain't been avoiding you."

"Haven't," he snapped as they reached the staircase and began to ascend it.

"Haven't what?"

"*Haven't* been avoiding you."

"I never said you had."

Drew almost groaned. Then he saw the sassy sparkle in Tori's eye and the grin dancing about her pretty lips, and knew she'd been playing him. His anger started to ease away.

"Where we going?"

"To someplace where we can be alone to…work."

Work. That's *all*. He was going to work with her. Not kiss her. Not throw her down onto the nearest flat surface and torture her with every sensual trick he knew until she admitted why she'd been avoiding him. Even though that's exactly what he wanted to do.

A thumping sound behind them reminded him why he couldn't. Looking back, he saw Jacey the camerawoman, strolling up the stairs, her camera on her shoulder. Drew glared at her, at the camera, at the television viewers who didn't even exist yet, but who were already getting in his way.

He considered taking Tori to his room, since it was the only place he felt pretty sure wasn't bugged. Then he thought better of it. Like it or not, they were on the set of a television show, and their every move was up for interpretation. If he hauled her into his bedroom right now, in a few months the entire television-watching public would be making up their minds about what had happened behind the closed door.

He couldn't do it to her.

"Come on," he said with a shake of his head, turning left at the top of the stairs, rather than right.

At the end of the hall, past the last bedroom door, the carpeted corridor widened into a small sitting area. It was somewhat secluded, overlooking the foyer through a railing on one side. The other was dominated by a window with a vista of the expansive east lawn. Two chairs stood in front of the window.

Leading her to one of the chairs, he dropped into the other one. He pulled it closer, until their knees almost touched. Jacey hadn't quite caught up yet so he leaned close and kept his voice low. "This isn't as private as the greenhouse, but it's the best we can do right now."

She nibbled on her lip. "About the greenhouse…"

"Yes?"

She looked over his shoulder, obviously spying the camerawoman. Jacey couldn't join them in the sitting area, it was too tiny. But she was taping them from a few feet away.

"Nothing," Tori muttered.

He followed her lead. "Good. You didn't lose the *g*."

"Pardon?"

"Did you make a noise?"

She laughed, a bright, joyous sound that spilled across her lips and washed over him like something sweet and clean. He began to relax for the first time all day.

"You're bad," she said. "Saucy."

"I think the saying 'it takes one to know one' might be appropriate here."

And it did. They were very much alike. He'd sensed that since the very beginning, even if she still hadn't realized it. "By the way, I was complimenting you on finishing the *ing* at the end of your word."

She grimaced. "Mr. Halloway, he's the kinda teacher who'd probably kept a switch in his desk back a hunnert years ago when he was teaching." Then she shook her head. "I mean a *hundred* years ago."

He noted the way she corrected herself, not a bit surprised at how quickly she was adapting to the changes in her daily life and dialect. "But you're doing well."

She nodded.

"And the rest of the classes?"

She shrugged, looking bored. "I suppose if Queen Elizabeth ever invites me over, I won't shock her by using my soup spoon to stir my tea."

The smart-alecky tone had returned to her voice, so at odds with the subdued way she'd behaved back in the kitchen.

"So what's the real reason you didn't come to my class?"

Her eyes shifted down, her half-lowered lashes concealing them from view. "Maybe I don't feel smart enough for current events yet."

"Yesterday," he said, his tone dry, "you missed a sparkling conversation on the Brad and Jen rumors. And today was even better, with everyone bringing up at least one topic they'd seen on a news program they were asked to watch last night." He couldn't help adding "I never knew *Entertainment Tonight* had such hard-hitting stories."

Her lashes came up. Those laughing blue eyes appeared again. "Are you going crazy yet?"

"Yeah. You?"

"Not so much. But we haven't really started doing a lot of the hard stuff yet."

He was almost afraid to ask. "What's the hard stuff?"

"Wearing fancy dresses."

Her grimace and tone would have been appropriate for someone who'd been invited to dine on monkey brains.

"I'll probably break my ankles if they make me wear any shoes higher than an inch."

"You found your *g*'s. You'll find your high-heel ankles."

Hearing a sound, he looked over his shoulder and saw Jacey capturing every word with her camera. She had a smile on her face. Not, he was surprised to note, a predatory one. But a rather nice one. As if she enjoyed Tori as much as he did.

He made a mental note to drop his dislike of the woman down one notch.

"Are you ready to get to work?" he asked Tori, trying to forget they were on camera.

"I didn't watch *Entertainment Tonight* last night." She nibbled her lip, looking almost guilty and tentative.

"No?" Then, knowing without a doubt what she had been doing, he leaned back in his chair and crossed his arms over his chest. "Okay then. Let's talk about *Tom Sawyer*."

5

JACEY TURNER HAD BEEN around enough to know attraction when she saw it. She might've had to have her *own* romance pointed out to her by Digg—who'd told her she was falling for him even before Jacey realized it herself—but she didn't have much trouble seeing it in other people.

And there was definitely something to see between Dr. Drew Bennett and race-car driver Tori Lyons.

"I'm telling you," she told director Niles Monahan, "Tori Lyons is the one."

The crew had gotten together for a week-one wrap meeting very early Sunday morning to discuss the latest round of cuts that had left them with nine contestants.

The director, a pale-faced whiner who had this really irritating, watery sniff after every third word he spoke, rolled his eyes. "You must be joking. She has such an awful twang."

"It's getting much better."

"She wore work boots beneath the Vera Wang gown we had her try on."

Jacey was with Tori on that one. She shot Niles a glare, ignoring the rest of the crew, who simply watched them argue yet again. Old news at this point. "You ever worn spike-heeled do-me shoes?" she asked.

His eyes bugged out and he sputtered a bit.

"They're agony." Jacey leaned back in her chair and crossed her legs, tapping her own black engineer boots, which she wore under her long, black wool skirt. "I'm sure as hell not going to criticize anybody else who doesn't wanna wear them, either."

Niles stared at her for a minute. She held his gaze until he finally looked away. She knew what he was thinking… He was wondering why he had to put up with an opinionated lead camera operator who his producer insisted be an active part of any decision making.

Niles didn't know Jacey was Burt's daughter. Which was exactly the way Jacey and Burt liked to keep things.

"That Ginny, she's looking good in her new wardrobe." This came from Spike, one of the guys on Jacey's camera crew, who had way too much testosterone and way too little intelligence.

"You mean you actually see her wardrobe? I thought you always pictured her naked," Jacey said with a roll of her eyes.

"I personally see the most potential in Robin," said Bernice, the makeup woman. "You know, she does her own face beautifully, and did from the day she walked in the door. I couldn't teach her a thing, if I were one of the instructors."

Personally, Jacey thought Robin wore so much makeup her whole face was being held together by it. If the layers of foundation ever came off, there might be a Kermit the Frog face under there. But she didn't want to offend Bernice, the only other woman on the crew, by saying so.

"It appears the field is wide open," Niles said with

a nod, as if everyone else's comments validated his lame opinions. "Of the nine women left, I'd say Tori Lyons isn't even in the top five in terms of her potential as lady of them all."

It was all Jacey could do not to yank her hair out by the fistful. "Are you all forgetting why we're *really* here?"

They all went silent, staring at her from around the meeting-room table where they'd ensconced themselves with coffee and bagels before the contestants came down.

"It's not about who *you* like the best. It's about who Dr. Bennett likes the best."

And that, Jacey knew without a doubt, was Tori Lyons.

"Well, I don't agree, but since three more have been eliminated, it will be easier to see his interaction with each of the women," Niles said, still sounding so superior.

But at least he was on the same wavelength, finally. "I've begun feeling him out about the necessity of interacting with the women in social settings," Jacey said. "And so has my f—Mr. Mueller, who called and spoke with him last night. That will be the perfect excuse to send him on dates." *Without him ever knowing he was dating.*

It was only fair to give the other women some one-on-one time with the hunky doc. Because so far, only Tori had had that chance, though, Jacey believed she was the only one on the set who knew Drew Bennett was sneaking out to meet with his star pupil every morning.

An early riser, Jacey had been making use of the treadmills in the fitness room of the house—a poor substitute for her morning run, but all she could manage. Yesterday and the day before, she'd seen Tori slipping out just after dawn, only to be followed by Drew. Both times, he'd had a book in his hand.

The Hollywood pessimist inside her speculated on what they were *really* doing together in the greenhouse. But the woman who saw the tender way he'd been helping Tori read some old book the other day suspected they were up to something altogether different. Which was why she hadn't ratted them out.

Not that it would matter, really, if she did. Because they met in the greenhouse—their blessing, but a camera's curse. Even if she had informed the snotty little director, what could he have done about it? If she or any of the crew showed up with a camera—after equipping it for the extreme moisture—Drew and Tori would likely stop their lessons altogether.

So she left them alone. Probably, she had to admit, because of the slight tinge of guilt she felt over her involvement in this whole thing. It had been her idea, after all. A part of Jacey felt a teeny bit bad about setting the good doctor up like this, even though the TV-insider part of her loved it.

Deep down, she'd also had a completely unexpected reaction, one Dr. Bennett—or her father—probably wouldn't believe. One she wouldn't have believed a few weeks ago, before this all began. But it was true. She'd gone all sappy and stupid because she saw something in Dr. Bennett's relationship with Tori that reminded her of her own. With Digg.

Jacey had been the wildly different outsider with the handsome, stoic fireman. She'd been where Tori was now. So a part of her wanted to see if Drew and Tori could possibly make it work. Because if they could, it might give her a renewed sense of faith for her own up-in-the-air romance. The one that, in spite of several tender long-distance phone calls this week, still seemed tenuous at best.

So as the meeting broke up and the crew separated for the day, she didn't even think of pointing Niles Monahan's attention toward the large window over the sideboard. She even intentionally blocked it with her body, to be sure nobody else saw what she'd just seen.

Drew and Tori, entering the greenhouse.

OF ALL THE ACTIVITIES that had filled her every waking moment for the past few days, Tori's favorite were these quiet mornings with Drew. They hadn't meant to do anything secret or sneaky, and she sure wasn't trying to get him alone so she could do any women's tricks on him. Unlike most of the other girls in the house.

He'd offered to help her with her reading. And she'd said yes. That's all there was to these daily meetings in the greenhouse.

Big fat liar. Yep. She was. Because that *wasn't* all there was to it. How could it be when she grew more and more attracted to him as each day passed?

She was changing. Not only in her speech—due to hard classes with frowny-faced old Mr. Halloway, who'd moved from getting her to pronounce her *g*'s to eliminating the word *ain't* from her daily speech. Not to mention doing whatever he could to soften up her accent. Shew, she hardly recognized her own voice sometimes.

The changes in her had sparked something else—a change in how she viewed *him.* Drew. Because every time she saw him, every time she spoke or displayed some of the knowledge she'd been picking up all week, he was there to look on in approval. Interest. Anticipation. As if he was, well, *waiting* for something. She only wished she knew what.

Their tutoring sessions were friendly and what-not, but as every day passed, she was more and more aware of this tension building between them. How could she not be when they were in this hot, humid place filled with moisture and heavenly smells? How could she possibly think of anything but having him kiss her again…and *more*…when they were together on a big, squishy, soft blanket they'd brought out from the house?

She told herself the blanket—which they hid in the storage closet each time they left—was so inviting only because it protected them from the ground. Not because it felt so wonderful to sprawl out here, lying on her stomach, right beside him.

Their bodies were just a few inches apart. Since he was sitting up, leaning against the storage closet, his legs right beside her, she was almost face level with his hip. Whoa, boy, had *that* given her some distracting moments. She sure would like to land in his lap again someday, like she had the night they'd met.

Forcing her thoughts away from the man's hard body, she tried to focus on the novel lying on the blanket in front of her. Propped up on her elbows, she read aloud from what was becoming her favorite book. "Is there really a book about Huckleberry Finn I could read after I finish this one?" she asked as she reached the end of the chapter.

"Yes. It's darker, lots of deeper themes about prejudice and hatred. But a good one. You'll be ready for it in no time."

"You keep teaching me tricks like the *i* before *e* one, or the one about two vowels going walking and the first one doing the talking, and you might be right."

He chuckled. "Tori, I'm sure you heard those silly rhymes in first grade."

"I didn't listen much in first grade."

"*That* I can believe."

She raised a brow. "You calling me a troublemaker?"

His wide-eyed expression looked innocent. "Oh, no. Why on earth would anyone think you're a troublemaker? Just because you led a hunger strike with your teammates to demand pizza for dinner Friday night instead of steak tartare."

She wrinkled her nose. "I'm supposed to be the one without social know-how, but I sure know better than to eat raw meat!"

He met her eye, laughing with her, but the laughter slowly faded. He kept looking at her, his dark eyes full of interest. Warmth. Steam. That coulda been the steam from the greenhouse. But she honestly didn't think the heat was coming from anywhere except him, this hot-as-blazes man.

The heavy moment was interrupted by a ringing sound. Drew reached into his pocket and withdrew a cell phone. Lucky him. Hers had been confiscated when she arrived on the set.

"Do you mind if I get this?" he asked after he checked the ID on the screen. "It's my sister."

She merely shrugged, then turned her attention back toward the book while he talked. She only heard his part of the conversation, but it wasn't hard to tell he doted on his sister. He was sweet and playful with her, teasing, the way Tori sometimes did with her baby brother Sammy. Then he grew more serious and began to frown.

She couldn't tell what was going on, but Drew didn't seem pleased with whatever he was hearing. Finally he said, "It's okay, Jill, I'll call him. He can't flunk you for that. But don't do it again."

After he'd disconnected the call, he dropped the phone back into his pocket. Feigning nonchalance, Tori asked, "Everything okay?"

He sighed heavily. "She finally went back to school, but she's been missing a lot of classes. One of her professors is threatening to flunk her out."

Tori nodded, still gazing at her book, not at Drew. Then she said evenly, "So you're gonna bail her out, huh? Seems to me if she's an adult she ought to be able to get out of her own problems."

That was all she had to say. A long moment of silence followed, before Drew laughed softly. "Okay," he admitted, "so we're both suckers. Maybe I won't call her professor and bail her out of this one."

"Good plan," she said, liking this additional proof that they were a lot more alike than she'd ever have expected at first.

"So tell me," he said, suddenly sounding more serious, "what have you heard about these *outings* we're supposed to have?"

She stiffened, unable to help it. She'd heard about what he called "outings." The director had called them "dates." Only none of the girls were supposed to tell Drew.

This was killing her, and she hated being reminded of why she was really here. For an hour or so every morning, here in the greenhouse, she was able to forget about everything else. Forget that inside the house were eight women ready to do just about anything—except maybe pop out of a cake naked—to get Drew's attention. And even the cake thing didn't sound too far-fetched for *some* of the girls, like Ginny and Teresa.

"I've heard," she mumbled, hating to have to keep the director's dirty little secret.

"Are you looking forward to them?"

She'd rather get a root canal than watch Drew Bennett walk out the door with one of the other women on his arm. If he kissed one'a them, she'd… she'd…well, she didn't know *what* she'd do. Probably punch something. Or somebody. Maybe even him.

"Are *you* looking forward to them?" she asked.

"Well, you know I don't want to be dragged on camera any more than absolutely necessary. I want as little to do with *Hey, Make Me Over* as possible." Then he shrugged, a tiny smile playing about his lips. "But I have to say, I don't mind the prospect of a few of them."

Tori had no experience playing coy, so she came right out and asked. "The ones with me?"

"Yeah."

"How come?"

He looked surprised by the question. "Well, it's a chance to be alone with you, outside of this place."

"With cameras and millions of TV viewers watching."

"We'll ignore them."

Impossible.

"I'm looking forward to dancing with you."

Her jaw dropped. "Dancing?"

"Of course. We're attending a holiday party at a local country club."

Tori scrunched her eyes closed and groaned. "I can't dance."

"Sure you can."

"No," she said, finally opening her eyes again. "Even the dance instructor is ready to declare me the two-left-feet girl."

"You can move your hands and feet in a race car with perfect precision, Tori. You're not clumsy."

Shrugging, she rolled her eyes. "That's natural."

"So's dancing," he said. "If you have the right partner."

"Meaning you?" She wondered if he heard that hopeful sound in her voice.

He nodded.

"I'll step all over your feet."

"You can't weigh much." His boyish grin didn't make her feel any better.

"I'll look stupid."

He brushed some hair off her face, his fingertips lingering on her cheek. "You'll look beautiful."

Gulping, she managed to whisper "I won't know what to do. The only dancing I know is line dancing in the honky-tonks. Or else slow dancing, which's more an excuse to make out while standing up than anything else. Girl's arms are around his neck, and the guy's hands are on her tush, and they just sorta stand there rubbing up against one another in time to the music."

Instead of replying, he rose to his feet, then bent down to offer her his hand. Tori put her fingers in his, letting him pull her to stand before him. She raised a brow, not sure whether he wanted to fold up the blanket to leave, or…something else. Then he drew her into his arms.

"What're you…"

"Dance with me," he murmured, holding her close.

Any protest she might have made faded right outta her mouth. She was back in his arms, exactly where she'd wanted to be for days. And oh, my, he felt wonderful.

The warmth in the greenhouse had made them both dress a little lighter for their mornings together. So now Tori wore a tight T-shirt with her jeans; Drew, a golf shirt. Tori had never considered her arms erogenous zones, but the brush of her bare skin against his had her rethinking that idea.

"There's no music," she murmured, not caring, hoping he didn't care, either.

"Sure there is," he said, lacing his fingers with hers, while his other hand, splayed against the small of her back, pulled her even closer. Until she gasped at the contact.

This, she realized, might be even *better* than the dancing she saw other couples doing in the darkness of the honky-tonks back home. He was still close, but it almost seemed proper, as if they were satisfying all the proprieties, but secretly flouting them at the very same time. She could enjoy this in public, she surely could. "Drew?"

"Shh. Close your eyes and feel it."

She closed her eyes, focusing on the warmth of his hands. The press of his firm chest against her nipples, which were taut and hard against her shirt. Never having a whole lot up top, Tori was in the habit of going without a bra, so the contact of her cotton shirt—not to mention his body—was especially sweet torture.

She couldn't help it. A teeny sigh escaped her lips as she fell into step with him, catching his rhythm as he moved to some unheard music. And suddenly, unbelievably, she almost *did* hear it. The hiss of the equipment, the whir of the overhead fan. The swish of the palms swaying under that breeze. Her heart provided a steadily pounding drumbeat and a bass note sounded with her every inhaled breath.

"There *is* music," she said, her eyes still closed as she turned her face to rest her cheek on his shoulder.

Their legs brushed against one another. Their hips moved together in about as intimate a touch as a body could have while clothed. But she didn't *want* to be clothed. She wanted to dance like this, upright, then, there on the blanket, without a bit of clothing between them.

He stopped moving. Tori slowly opened her eyes to see that smooth, hot skin of his neck so very close. She had to taste it. Without a word, she rose on tiptoe and pressed her lips to a vulnerable spot just below his ear.

He hissed. He didn't, however, pull away. Which left her free to explore a little with her mouth. She pressed soft kisses down toward his shoulder, then moved to the front, licking a bit at the hollow of his throat.

"Tori," he groaned.

"Kiss me, please," she whispered, her voice sounding breathy and full of need.

And he did. Lifting her chin with the tips of his fingers, he lowered his lips to hers, catching her mouth in a slow, wet, hungry kiss. A deep sigh came from her throat as he licked her tongue, tasting her with delicate precision. Achingly slow and so intimate she felt as if she was being appreciated like some of that fancy wine she'd been learning about all week.

Then he started to move. To dance again. To slide his hard form against hers while both his hands dropped to her hips. She didn't protest when he slipped them below the bottom of her shirt and lifted it. Didn't even breathe when he tugged it all the way off and tossed it aside. Thought ceased altogether when he ran those big, strong hands of his up her sides to tease the bottoms of her breasts.

He finally pulled away, just far enough to look down at her, his eyes filled with dark desire. "You're gorgeous."

She didn't answer. Instead, she reached for his shirt. He helped her pull it up and off. "So're you."

Then their mouths met again and their dance continued. Only now, their upper bodies touched, slid against each other and aroused Tori to the brink of insanity. The heat and humidity caused a sheen of moisture on their skin, reducing friction. Raising awareness.

"See? Dancing's easy."

"Think anyone'll notice at that fancy party if we dance naked?" she asked with a sigh.

A low rumble of laughter was his only reply. But his hands were busy, cupping her, teasing her, tweaking her nipples with his fingertips as they continued their sultry dance.

Tori held her breath as he bent lower to taste the skin of her neck, down to her collarbone. When he dropped to his knees in front of her, she couldn't help swaying into him, until he encircled her thighs with one powerful arm. He tasted her belly, her torso, until Tori was whimpering with the need to have his mouth on one of her begging-for-attention nipples.

"Drew," she wailed, bending toward him practically ordering him to give her what she hungered for.

He finally took pity and covered the tip of her breast with his lips. One strong pull and she cried out, having to rest her hands on his bare shoulders to support herself on suddenly shaky legs. She felt the sensation rushing through her body, almost not recognizing it because it'd never been so powerful before.

She was dying for him. Just *dying.* Every flick of his tongue against her breast sent bolts of delight downward, until the throbbing between her legs was almost unbearable. When he moved his mouth away, she immediately dropped down to her knees, right in front of him. Their lips met again in a hot, quick mating, and she reached for his belt.

He said something, leaning away. It took a second for her to realize what it had been.

"Tori, no...."

"I want this," she whispered, reassuring him even as she nipped and sucked at his neck.

"So do I."

She went for the belt again.

"But not now."

She froze, her fingers just barely brushing the front of his pants, where his visible erection strained against the fabric. "You wanna run that by me again?"

He closed his eyes and gave one hard shake of his head, as if trying to knock some sense back into it. If he continued with this crazy talk, he was gonna get some help.

"God, if only you knew how hard this is for me."

"*It's* hard for *me*," she insisted, staring directly at his crotch. "I can *see* how hard it is for me."

A hoarse laugh that sounded more pained than amused erupted from his lips. "You're not ready," he finally said.

Oh, she was ready, all right. "Wanna bet?" she snapped. Then she proved it to him by grabbing his hand and pulling it down her body. Down over the front of her jeans.

Right between her legs where the fabric was hot and damp.

He shuddered, cupping her, his eyes closing as a groan of male pleasure eased from his mouth. Tori shook a little, arching into his hand, desperate to have him touch her naked skin, but also loving the anticipation and friction caused by her jeans.

"Any more questions?" she asked, not needing an answer. Reaching up, she laced her fingers into his hair and tugged him close for another slow, wet kiss, knowing he couldn't claim she didn't really want him when her own body insisted she did.

Then he pulled away. Both his mouth, *and*, dangitall, his hand. "We can't."

"Argh," she groaned, "how could I be any more ready?"

"Okay, I'*m* not ready for this."

This time she reached for the front of *his* pants. "News flash, Professor. I got a fistful here that calls you a liar," she managed to say between harsh breaths as she closed her hand over him. All of him. Sakes alive, every hard, throbbing bit of him.

His jaw started clenching as the pulse in his temple pounded. But when she caressed him, leaning up to kiss him at the same time, he turned his head away.

"This can't happen, Tori. Not now."

She'd seen that look on his face before. That stern, hard look, so different from his usual friendly self. And she finally realized he meant what he said.

Disappointment flooded through her as she dropped to sit on her bent legs. It was followed by a quick flash of anger. "There's a name they call women who do what you just did."

He gaped. "You're calling me a…tease?"

"Uh-huh."

He sat back, too, thrusting a hand into his hair, then looking up in the air as if somebody up there had answers she wasn't privy to. Then he met her eye, his jaw clenched still, making it clear he wasn't at all calm. "I didn't mean to tease you. It went too far." Sighing deeply, he added, "If it's any help, I'm suffering, too. I want you so much I'm going to have to take a cold shower after we leave here so I can get control of myself."

His confession didn't help. "Well, in case you didn't know it, Mr. Professor, cold showers don't work so great for women." Reaching for her shirt, she let her tongue rush ahead of her brain. "I ain't exactly the type to take care of business on my own. Even if I were, I sure don't have the privacy of my own bedroom, with no cameras. So I'm gonna be walking around for the next two weeks dying to come and not able to do it."

Tori paused, her blood rushing to her face as she realized what she'd just said. She'd never once, in her life, talked to a man about something like…that. She'd hardly ever *done*…that. Touching herself.

Realizing she'd said it out loud—put those

thoughts, those images, in both their heads—she dropped her shirt and clenched her hands together. Closing her eyes, she bit her lip and waited, praying she'd hear the opening—and closing—of the greenhouse door. *Go, just go.*

She didn't hear anything for a long moment, only the pounding of her heart and the deep breaths she inhaled to try to calm herself.

"Well," he finally said, his voice thick and hoarse, "we can't have that, now can we?"

DREW HAD WANTED TORI from the first moment he saw her. Maybe back then, he would have gone for something more physical if he'd had the chance—without cameras present. But now, he was falling for her. More interested in her than he'd been in anyone for a long time. Which had instantly sent up warning flares in his brain.

He couldn't help thinking of his long-ago engagement. Of how his former fiancée had changed overnight from the girl next door, who wanted to marry him and have babies, to the pouting wannabe-actress who'd flown to Hollywood and hitched up with the first millionaire she'd met.

He wouldn't say she'd broken his heart, but she'd put a dent in it. One he was reminded of now, with Tori. Because, he sensed, he really *could* care for her, in a way he never had about anyone else.

So he couldn't act on his desire for her. Not until she knew what she wanted, where she was going, and where he might fit into the picture. Not until she was ready for it, in every way.

She might be *physically* ready now. Oh, God, yeah, she was physically ready. His whole body nearly shook remembering how hot and damp and needy she'd been.

But in every other way, she was far from it.

He couldn't become her lover until she recognized and dealt with the changes in her life. Tori hadn't yet grasped what was happening here. She hadn't realized she was doing a hell of a lot more than competing for some new clothes and jewelry. She was striding forward into a new future.

Soon, as she continued to gobble up every bit of knowledge she could, as her hungry, bright mind strove further and further toward new experiences, she'd reach a point of no return—when she came to understand she couldn't return to her old world. Not entirely. Nor would she *want* to go back to it.

Who knew what new world she'd want. Hell, for all he knew, it could be one in Hollywood, with oily plastic surgeons.

So no, better to keep at least some kind of distance between them. At least for now, until she figured out for sure that she wanted a *lover,* not just a hot sexual encounter. And that she wanted a real future, not a step back into her small-town world where she couldn't even read a book in peace.

When she reached that moment, he planned to be by her side to help her deal with it. And *then* to act on the hot desire he'd felt for her from day one. When she was ready—*really* ready—he was going to make love to her until they'd both die from pleasure.

But now? No. He couldn't take her now, couldn't bury himself inside her and lose his mind, not when Tori had no idea who she'd be—or what she'd want—next week.

He *could*, however, give her some relief, temporary though it might be.

"Drew?" she asked, confusion in her voice.

"Shh," he said, staring at her, drawing in a few deep breaths to be sure he had control of himself. He couldn't touch her until he did. So instead, he simply waited. And stared.

She was glorious. Her body damp and misty from the humid air and the passionate heat they'd made each other feel. Sitting just a few inches away in jeans and nothing else, she looked almost pagan, with her long, curly hair curtaining one breast. The other was completely bare, and his mouth went dry, remembering how she'd tasted, the little coos she'd made when he'd sucked her pretty, taut nipple.

Finally, reminding himself that a cold shower and his own hand would do him okay later on, he moved close to her again. "I'm not going to have sex with you right now."

She opened her mouth to protest, but he put his hand up, palm out, stopping her. With a wicked grin, he promised, "But I *can* give you lots of nice things to think about…until we do."

Her eyes flared a bit and her pink tongue slipped out to moisten her lips. Drew needed no further invitation. He dropped his mouth to hers, open and hungry, licking her, nearly devouring her.

"Lie back," he ordered.

She instantly complied.

Drew kissed her again, making love to her mouth with deep, steady thrusts of his tongue, while his hand roamed over her. Cupping one breast, he caught her nipple between his fingertips and teased it until she began to whimper.

"Please…"

She didn't have to ask twice. Kissing his way down her body, he covered her breast with his mouth, then sucked deep. At the same moment, he dropped one hand between her legs and cupped her through her jeans, the pressure of his palm hitting her at just the right angle.

She bucked up against him, crying out again. "Touch me, touch me," she began to murmur. "Closer, please."

Though he'd hoped to keep the physical barrier of clothing between them, his own pants would have to do. Because he could no more deny her than he could stop drawing short choppy breaths into his lungs. She took the matter out of his hands, literally, by reaching down to unfasten her own jeans and push them down over her hips.

Drew tasted his way down her body, with kisses and light nips of his teeth, until he reached the top of her tiny panties.

"Up," he murmured as he slid his hands beneath her bottom to lift her. She helped, making it easy for him to tug her jeans farther down and out of the way. Then he swept her panties away in one smooth stroke, pausing for a second to appreciate her secret, feminine beauty.

Her body was lean and smooth, her skin a perfect creamy color, soft and supple. She had a tiny little birthmark on her right hip, and he ran his fingers over it, wanting to taste her there. Everywhere.

She arched up, rising toward him, knowing what was coming and *wanting* it.

With a helpless groan of pleasure, Drew dropped his lips over her, tasting her sweet hot flesh. Her warm scent filled his head, until he only vaguely heard her cries of pleasure. Her body rocked, finding its rhythm, which he matched with his tongue. And, unable to resist, his fingers, which he sunk inside her.

He groaned at the sensations battering him. Glorious. She was absolutely glorious. Wet, soft, welcoming around his fingers and beneath his mouth. The urge to unzip his pants and plunge into her, to lose himself in that tight warmth nearly made him lose his mind. Not to mention his control.

Thank God Tori had nearly lost hers. Her cries of pleasure pierced the haze of lust in his brain, giving him the strength to proceed with *just* his hand and tongue.

"Yes, Drew, yes," she cried, her voice shaky and trembling.

"Come now, Tori," he growled as he picked up the pace, knowing he had to take her up and over the edge soon or risk going over it with her.

And finally, perfectly, she did.

6

AFTER THEIR INTERLUDE in the greenhouse, Drew no longer trusted himself to be alone with Tori—at least, not unless they were within sight of a camera. If he allowed himself to be *completely* alone with her again—without a video chaperone—there would be no stopping. Not until they'd both achieved the kind of shattering climax he'd been able to give her Sunday morning. He'd completely lose the thin thread of control that'd kept him from making love to her then.

So it was time to end their reading lessons in the greenhouse.

Tori seemed to understand, without him having to say a word. Since that morning, she'd been subdued around him, quiet and watchful. As if waiting for him to decide what he wanted. That was a no-brainer. He wanted her. In any way he could have her. Preferably in *every* way he could have her.

Not now, asshole, he reminded himself, trying to remember exactly why his stupid intellect had been in control over his body Sunday when she'd so obviously wanted more.

Then he remembered. It was because she was changing. Growing. Emerging like a butterfly from a cocoon every single day.

The twangy southern accent was smoother now.

Still detectable, but softened, until her voice sounded nearly lyrical. Her eyes still sparkled, but those raucous witticisms didn't fall off her pretty lips as often. She wore the same casual clothes, but wore them a little better—because her chin was high and her shoulders straight. She looked more confident, that was the only way he could describe it.

Confident. Beautiful. Nearly irresistible.

He'd also been fascinated to learn Tori had an amazing memory. Now, with her newfound confidence, she'd reached the point where she debated with him about current issues during their daily classes, nailing names, dates and details with almost photographic precision. The other women in the group just watched, wide-eyed and wide-mouthed while the two of them shot different opinions back and forth.

There was no question: every day brought her closer to the new woman she was going to be. A new woman who might not even *want* to get involved with him. So he waited it out, missing their private time together, wondering how the hell he'd ever thought a cold shower and his own hand were going to be enough to sate the incredible want.

He was about to lose his mind from sexual tension. God, Tori merely had to walk into the room in her tight jeans that hugged her pert little ass and he reacted as predictably as Pavlov's dog. He'd taken to keeping books, newspapers or papers in his lap whenever he knew she was about to show up. He could only hope some eagle-eyed old lady out in TV land didn't notice and lodge an indecency complaint with the network. He could see the tabloid headlines now: Man Unable To Keep It Down. And below:

Passes Out On National TV From Lack Of Oxygen To The Brain. His picture would be right next to the one of the latest martian robot clone who looked just like Richard Simmons.

"Get your mind outta your pants, man," he whispered aloud as he sat in his room Thursday morning. "Mind over body."

That basic philosophy seemed to have deserted him. His emotions had twisted him up inside, and his intellect seemed to have abandoned him as he got wrapped tighter and tighter in this reality-show noose.

Though Tori was the cause of his most basic problem—an overactive libido—she was also the only pleasure he had in this madhouse. He wanted her like crazy, but he also truly *liked* her. He liked spending time with her, and her presence was just about the only thing he looked forward to every single day. So he put up with the sensual torture if only to gain the emotional relief.

They hadn't stopped the reading lessons altogether, they'd simply moved them indoors. For an hour each day, they sat together in the open area in the upstairs hall, where they'd sat the first time they'd read *Tom Sawyer,* in full view of the camera and the crew.

It hadn't taken long for the other girls to find out he was giving Tori private lessons. It seemed to annoy them for some reason, because suddenly he was being asked to help Ginny with her geography and Robin with her world politics. And he'd probably soon hear from Teresa who'd say she needed to learn…well, probably whatever she could about poles. North, south or brass.

As long as it wasn't *his*, he really didn't care.

The women's nonstop attention had gone beyond tiresome to outright annoying. Drew liked women. Hell, he'd been crazy about a few of them in his life. But he preferred to choose his own, *not* have them chase him down like he was the fox to their hounds. He'd seen less-determined grad students.

As the week went on, it became harder and harder to leave his own unwired room without stumbling over one of them clad in a skimpy robe, or another asking him to help her fix something in her room. Like he was stupid enough to get himself trapped in a bedroom with one of them? Christ, he'd be safer pulling up a chair next to a vampire than letting one of these women get him alone.

Which was why he was spending nearly every spare minute he had locked inside his room, like now, as he sat by the window looking outside, counting the hours until he could get out of here. A soft knock interrupted his contemplation of the snowy lawn, and made him stop wondering if he could make snowshoes out of tennis rackets and escape on foot.

"Yes?" he asked, knowing better than to actually unlock the door again. Last time, he'd ended up with a face full of Tiffany's breasts, barely covered by a skimpy bikini. She'd asked him to join her in the hot tub. He'd told her he was allergic to water.

Somehow, he couldn't even claim too much surprise that she'd believed him.

"Drew? It's me. Tori."

Her voice got his immediate attention. He undid the lock, opened the door and drank her in with his eyes. She'd started dressing differently, due to the influence of the show, he suspected. He liked the pale pink sweater draping softly across her curves, and the beige slacks that emphasized them even more. But the naughtiness in her eye—that hadn't changed a bit. She was still the saucy, outrageous woman she'd been on the day of her arrival.

Thank God in heaven.

"I need your help," she said. "Can I come in?"

Come in. Into his bedroom. Where there were no cameras. But there *was* a bed. A big comfortable bed.

And him with the same hard-on he'd had for going on four days now.

No. She definitely could *not* come in.

But somehow, his upper brain lost control over his vocal cords. Because it was surely the one below his belt that answered, "Sure."

TORI COULD HAVE COME UP with any number of excuses to see Drew over the past few days, but she hadn't. The man had made it very clear he needed his space. Needed to figure things out before they went any further. She had to give him what he'd asked for, even if it nearly killed her since she was dying for more of the same wicked delights he'd shown her Sunday.

But today, she really did need his help. A few more orgasms would be dang nice, too, but she wasn't one to be greedy.

"I've been worrying about Luther," she explained as she stepped into Drew's room. She glanced around in curiosity. This was the first time she'd come into his room. To her knowledge, it was the first time *any* of the women on the set had been allowed into his room, which made it easier for her to sleep at night.

"Your brother?" Drew asked as he shut the door, then turned to face her.

Tori nodded. "We're not allowed to contact any-one in the outside world. But ever since I saw you talking on your cell phone Sunday, I've been think-ing maybe the rules didn't apply to you."

Drew crossed his arms and leaned against the doorjamb, looking sexy as all get-out. He hadn't shaved yet, and his face had a bit of a morning shadow. And he wore—lord have mercy—jeans. Tight jeans that hugged those lean hips and rode below his flat belly. His pullover shirt was long-sleeved, but not loose and baggy. Nope, it was tight, accentuating every inch of his broad chest and his thick arms.

But it was his bare feet that made her legs start to wobble. Lord, this man had it all. From the top of his tousled hair to the bottom of his sexy feet, he was temptation walking.

Tori gulped, then turned her attention toward the window.

"You want to borrow my phone?" he asked, ap-parently not noticing the look of dumb lust washing over her face.

She shook her head. "No, I don't wanna cheat." She said that part for the cameras because, truly, if she could call home herself, she would. "But I was thinking maybe *you* could call for me."

She heard him step closer, but still didn't turn around.

"And say what?"

"You don't have to say noth—anything. Just dial the number, ask for Luther, and see if he's there. If they say he's in the hospital or the morgue or some-thing, I guess I'll have my answer. Or if he gets on and sounds like he's talking through a buncha band-ages or a busted-up face, I'll know, too."

Her flip tone didn't hide her worry. She realized he'd heard it when he put a hand on her shoulder. "I'm sure he's fine. And I thought we made a pact not to interfere with our siblings who need to grow up."

"I'm not interfering," she said, "I'm curious, is all." She ducked away, still not turning around. My, oh my, her whole shoulder felt hot where his hand had rested on it for that brief second. She probably had a glow-in-the-dark red handprint there, right on her sweater, for all the TV world to see. "I'd feel better if I knew for sure." Clearing her throat, she raised her voice. "But I sure don't aim to cheat."

Drew paused. During the moment of silence, Tori nibbled her lip, then slowly turned around to peek at him through half-lowered lashes. He was smiling, a small secretive smile. "You think there are cameras in here, don't you?"

Rolling her eyes, she fisted one hand and put it on her hip. "Well, duh."

Raising his arms to his sides, he gestured around the room. "It's clean. I know how to spot hidden cameras…. Why do you think the pictures are off the walls and the grates for the heating vents are missing? My deal gave me complete privacy behind that door. My private life is off-limits." Crossing his arms, he added, "But I'm not stupid. I check *every* time I come back in this room."

They both glanced at the door. The firmly closed door. And the tension in the room ratcheted up. Tori drew a shaky breath into her lungs as she realized the implications. They had complete privacy. As in, she could strip off her clothes and jump up and down naked to get his attention, and nobody else would ever know.

He must have seen the thought dash through her brain because he took a tiny step back. "That doesn't mean…"

"Yeah, I know," she muttered, shaking her head in disgust.

"Forget it. I didn't come in here for that, anyway. I came to ask you to call Luther for me." Then she remembered what he'd said. "But if there's no cameras, maybe I could use your phone after all."

He shook his head. "No." Then he reached for a pen and paper on the table next to his bed. "But if you write down the number, I'll call and see if he's able to come to the phone. That'll tell you something. Will that satisfy you?"

She snorted at the way he put that while she wrote down the number. "Satisfy me? Huh. You should know better than anyone what satisfies me."

Drew closed his eyes. She could practically hear him counting to ten, and almost regretted taunting him again. She definitely regretted it when he responded with a throaty whisper. "If that's all it takes I'm gonna have a great time satisfying you over and over again until you can't even remember your own name."

Tori gasped. She hadn't expected such a sexy reaction.

He gave her a pitying little smile. "But not now."

She wanted to throttle him. "Right. You're still not gonna finish what you started Sunday morning. Same old story."

He quirked a brow and frowned. "You calling me a tease again?"

She merely shrugged. He was the one who'd put the name on it.

"Because, if I'm not mistaken, you were the *only* one who walked out of the greenhouse Sunday morning feeling any sort of…relief."

Heat flooded her cheeks. Darn the man for saying it out loud, as if it wasn't already embarrassing enough to think about the fact that he'd seen her most private parts—pretty close up—and she hadn't seen him with so much as his belt unbuckled.

She could, however, remedy that.

"Ahh, ahh," he said with a shake of his head, as soon as she began reaching for him.

"Maybe I was going for your phone," she snapped.

"Maybe you were going for my zipper." His half smile dared her to deny it.

"Maybe a *normal* man would wish I was."

His eyes flared a bit, and his smile tightened. A funny throbbing started in his temple and she knew he was gritting his teeth, trying to hold on to his casual laughter and his laid-back attitude.

Her respect for him went up a notch. Not one other man in Tori's life had ever been very successful at keeping control of his temper. This one was.

"Don't ever doubt I'm a normal man, Tori," he warned, his deep breaths and tight tone the only indications of his anger. "I've been picturing you naked and open to me every minute of every day this week."

Her heart tripped a little in her chest.

"I see your face when I close my eyes at night and I dream of burying myself inside you, making love to you until you have to scream at how good it feels." He stepped closer, lifting her chin with the tip of his finger to make good and sure he had her attention. As if she was capable of tearing it away from his husky voice and the wicked word-pictures he was painting.

"I want to *devour* you again."

Oh, mercy.

"I've never tasted anything as sweet and wet as your body and I've been hungry for more," he whispered, sounding like a starving man. "I want to feel your mouth on me, too, and I want us to do every erotic, wicked thing we can think of together."

She drew in a jagged breath, turning her face in his palm until she could press a kiss against his warm skin. Her tongue flicked out to taste him, just a tiny bit of him. He moved his hand, tangling his fingers into her hair and tilted her head back. "Oh, Tori," he muttered, as if unable to help himself. Then he kissed her, his mouth consuming her, giving and taking until, as he'd threatened, she couldn't even remember her own name.

When he pulled away, she had to keep her eyes closed, trying to bring the world back into focus as she swayed on unsteady legs. Finally, when she felt capable of thought, she managed one word. One single word. "When?"

He hesitated for a moment, until she opened her eyes and looked at him. The stark, raw want on his face mirrored her own.

"When you can tell me you understand exactly *why* I waited."

Then he turned toward the door and walked out of his own room, leaving her there, alone.

"YOU READY TO GO, Professor?" Drew heard as he stood by the front door, ready to go on another of these ridiculous "outings" Saturday night. This time, he was escorting a small group of the women—Tiffany, Sukie and Robin—to the ballet.

So far, none of the outings had been one-on-one. Which suited him fine. At least, until Sunday evening when he was supposed to escort Tori to the local country club for a holiday dance. Then, if disaster struck and two of the girls came down with mysterious ailments, leaving just him and Tori, he wouldn't complain a bit. Because in spite of the agony of being alone with her while unable to make love to her, he missed her too damn much to stay away from her.

She hadn't shown up for her private reading lesson yesterday or today. After Thursday's interlude in his bedroom, he hadn't been entirely surprised. The only time they'd talked was very briefly before the other women had arrived for their current events class, when he'd told her about his call to Luther.

Tori had been relieved to hear her brother hadn't sounded bandaged, drugged or in pain. Not that Drew had engaged him in a conversation or anything. He'd simply asked for the man, gotten him on the line, then offered him a subscription to *Ladies' Home Journal*.

Tori's brother had hung up so fast, Drew's ear had stung.

"Professor?"

"I'm ready," he said as he watched the three women descend the stairs.

They were all dressed appropriately—courtesy of Evelyn, the hair, makeup and clothing instructor. Still, in this case, the clothes definitely didn't make the women. With these three, he had to wonder what the evening had in store. They'd probably be lucky not to land in jail, though, that was less likely since

Ginny wouldn't be along to flash anyone. And Teresa wouldn't be there to gyrate against any light poles.

"So this ballet, it's called *The Nutcracker?*" Tiffany asked.

Drew nodded, already dreading the evening ahead. He hated the ballet. Really, truly hated it. But he hadn't been given much choice. Apparently all the instructors were going on public outings with the students, who'd been narrowed down to six yesterday morning.

One interesting thing to note—he and all the other instructors appeared to be completely in agreement on which women were doing the best with their "makeovers." The women Drew had ranked the highest had all advanced into the next round of play. They were falling faster now. By Monday, there would be four, and Wednesday would reveal the final two. These little "tests" and the women's performance in their daily classes would determine the winner in this *Pygmalion* game.

He had no doubt who would win. Tori was thriving, practically glowing with energy and light. Her speech was beautiful, her manners graceful. Sure, she had a few rough spots, but she, more than anyone, had made the most dramatic change in the past two weeks.

He tried to remain impartial and had to admit that Robin had done pretty well, too. And Sukie had tried awfully hard. As for the rest? Well, he doubted any of them would be around come Tuesday.

It was just his bad luck he'd drawn the ballet outing. He'd have much preferred taking the women to a ball game or even a singles' club…a place where they could get their kicks making plays for *other* men for a change.

Because *he* was getting damned tired of it.

"Drew?" Tiffany prompted. "We're going to see something called *The Nutcracker?*"

"Exactly."

"And it's a Christmas story?" Sukie asked.

This time Robin answered. "Haven't you two ever heard of *The Nutcracker?*"

"Is it anything like the *Terminator?* Because, I really liked those movies, I think they'd make great dancing shows," Tiffany said.

Drew closed his eyes. *God give me strength.* "No, Tiffany, it's nothing like the *Terminator.*"

"Well, who's the nutcracker? Is she a superhero or something? Or a cop? Does she really crack the nuts of the guys on stage, or is it just pretend, like WWE wrestling?"

"I'll explain it on the way," he murmured, shaking his head in tired resignation as he led the ladies out to the waiting car.

He only hoped that whatever Tori was doing this evening would be more interesting than what he had in store.

"TURN OFF THE CAMERA and get drunk with me."

Tori watched a smile curve Jacey Turner's lips up at the corners. The camerawoman looked younger— nicer—when she smiled. Not nearly so goth, with her black clothes and pale skin. In fact, Tori realized for the first time, Jacey was probably only her age, younger than she'd originally thought.

"I really shouldn't," Jacey said, sounding regretful.

"Oh, criminy," Tori muttered as she stalked across the library to the bar. "We have the place to ourselves. It ain't...it's *not*...like you're going to have to catch every minute of somebody batting her eyelashes or shaking her tail feathers at the professor."

She couldn't prevent a frown at that one. Lord it was driving her batty to watch the women in this place throwing themselves at him. And Drew, God love the man's soul, had thrown every one of them back, untouched, so far.

Except her. Tori. Her he'd touched. And kissed. And tasted. And stuck his tongue into….

Enough of that, she reminded herself with a hard shake of the head. She couldn't go there, not even in her own mind. Not without getting all weak and shaky remembering those wildly erotic moments Sunday and the intensely sexual conversation they'd had in his room Thursday morning.

"This place is empty, isn't it?" Jacey admitted.

It was. They were pretty much alone. Drew had, to Tori's complete annoyance, taken a trio of women out to the ballet. Tori and the remaining two—Teresa and Ginny—were supposed to go on a shopping trip with Evelyn, who was teaching them all about beauty and fashion. Tori had played hooky, pretending she had a stomachache. Tori didn't suppose she'd mind, since Evelyn had latched on to Robin as her most promising pupil. That was probably because Robin knew more about women's makeup than Mary Kay. And had more of it.

"You're not sick, are you?" Jacey asked, still not putting the camera down.

Tori stuck her tongue out at it. "Nope. You gonna tell on me?"

Chuckling, the other woman hit a switch on her camera and the lens came out a little bit. Tori stuck her tongue out again, this time not only at Jacey, but at all of the TV-watching public, who might be seeing this moment on close-up in a couple of months.

"You just confessed in front of half of America."

"Yeah, well, as long as Miss Evelyn doesn't find out till I'm long gone, back in Tennessee, I don't much care." Tori poured herself a shot—some good Kentucky bourbon—and raised a glass, not to mention a questioning brow. "You in? You know you do deserve a break once in a while."

Nodding, Jacey turned the camera off and lowered it to her side. "Straight up."

"My kinda gal," Tori said, pouring another neat shot of bourbon. Handing it to Jacey, she lifted her own for a toast. "To getting that camera out from in front of your pretty face."

Jacey snorted a laugh. "To stomachaches and an empty house."

"And no more lame-ass reality shows," Tori said with a disgusted sigh. Then she lifted the glass to her lips and drained it. The warmth fell into her belly, then spread out all through her body, bringing instant—if short-lived—calm. "Good."

"Very," Jacey said.

"I wonder if Mr. Mueller has to pay the owners of this house for this stuff."

"Serves him right if he does," Jacey said. "It's the least he can do since he took off, leaving the rest of us here to suffer."

Tori poured them each another shot. "So," she asked, "you like your job following people around trying to catch 'em at their worst for the sake of ratings?"

Jacey raised a brow and took her drink. "I like what I do. Reality TV is just part of it."

"The hellacious part?"

Snorting, Jacey nodded, then sat down on one of the cushy leather sofas. "This one has been pretty bad. But the last one...well, it had its moments."

Seeing the secretive smile on the other woman's face, Tori chuckled. "I can picture what kind of moments."

Jacey lifted her feet onto the coffee table, tugging her long, thick skirt out of the way. "Murder, mayhem, love, sex, lots of fun stuff."

Tori gaped. "You serious?"

As the other woman nodded, Tori whistled a little. Then she figured it out. "You were on the set of *Killing Time In A Small Time,* the murder-mystery show, weren't you?"

Again Jacey nodded.

"Wow," Tori mumbled. "The right guy won for a change." Then, thinking about who the winner had been, she asked, "Is Digg as much of a hottie in real life as he is on TV?"

Jacey didn't answer right away. Instead she drained her glass, then stood and approached the bar to help herself to another. Finally she muttered, "He is."

There was a story there, but Tori wasn't about to pry to get at it. Prying in other people's business left them feeling a mite bit too free to pry into her own. And as much as she was enjoying Jacey's company tonight, she wasn't about to forget the woman's job was to try to find out every little bit of information she could about Drew Bennett and any potential lovers.

Of course, they weren't lovers. Not technically, anyway. Though, she honestly had to say that any man who'd had his tongue where *his* had been had probably earned the right to be called a wee bit more 'n a friend.

"Ready?" Jacey asked, holding the bottle up.

Tori shook her head. She might have joined Jacey in another drink, but, truly, Tori didn't have much of a head for bourbon. So instead, she moved right to club soda, which she sipped and nursed for an hour or more. As they talked, she began to really like Jacey. The other girl was caustic, with a kind of pull-no-punches wit that Tori had always admired in others. Though on the surface they had nothing in common, she found herself thinking she and Jacey could become good friends. Jacey even talked her into getting back to doin' some drinkin', and Tori was working on a nice little head buzz after another shot.

"So," the camerawoman said after they'd discussed everything from their childhoods to the best—and worst—of the reality-TV craze, "tell me how you think it's going."

"What's going?"

"This show. How will it go down in the annals of reality-TV history?"

Tori grunted. "No brainer. As a big lust-fest with an audience who hates every woman in this place and roots for the professor to tell all you TV folks to take this show and shove it when he finds out the truth."

Jacey stared, her mouth dropping open. "Well, gee, don't pull any punches. Tell me what you really think."

"I call 'em like I see 'em."

And she did. She wasn't exaggerating one bit. She hoped when it came right down to it, and Drew learned he'd been misled and lied to, that he'd walk out of here without a backward glance for any one of them.

A twist of pain in her gut called her a liar, since she suspected she'd want a lot more than a backward glance. Tori chalked it up to the bourbon, refusing to allow herself to dream there was any possibility of a future between them.

"You really want him to walk away without falling in love?"

"He ain't gonna fall in love with any of these women," she muttered, dropping back into her Tennessee accent. "He's smart and he's well traveled and he's drop-dead gorgeous. What's a single woman on this set have to offer a man like that?"

Jacey stared her directly in the eye, her smile fading away. Then she leaned forward in her seat, dropping her elbows on her knees. "How about a great woman who's funny and smart and brave as hell. One who makes him laugh and makes him hot and will make anyone with a brain and two good eyes root for her to succeed?"

It took Tori a second to realize who the other woman was talking about. When she did, she snorted. "Not a chance."

"Yes, there is."

"Uh-uh," Tori said, shaking her head in disbelief. "Drew Bennett's got about as much chance of falling in love with me as I got of being named lady of them all in some real-life fairy tale." Tori flung herself back in her overstuffed chair, her legs sprawled out in very unladylike fashion in front of her. Miss Evelyn would likely have a conniption. But tonight, Tori just plum didn't care. "Besides which, even if he did start caring for somebody, me or Ginny or you for that matter, the minute he finds out he's been lied to and made a fool of on national TV, those feelings'll die pretty fast."

Jacey's brow pulled down in an obvious frown. She thought it over, then perked back up. "That might be his first reaction. But the hero always comes around when true love is involved."

The words *hero* and *true love* didn't seem the type to fall too easily off Jacey's lips. That's how Tori knew the girl'd had one too many shots.

"Believe me," Tori said, rolling her eyes at the romantic picture Jacey painted, "Drew's no Prince Charming, and I'm sure no fairy-tale princess. I'd never *want* to be. I wanted to smack Snow White when I saw that movie as a kid. Imagine taking an apple from someone who looked like that old witch. Girl didn't have a lick of sense in her purty little head."

Jacey nodded, understanding perfectly. "I wanted Sleeping Beauty to march herself right to her parents and tell them off for dumping her on three fairy godmothers in some godforsaken cabin. Cripes, they were the frickin' king and queen. Couldn't they have at least sent her to some fabulous boarding school on the Mediterranean?"

The two of them giggled as they continued to trash fairy-tale princesses. Tori figured Walt Disney had to be rolling over in his grave, right there along with those Grimm brothers. As they talked, she thought again about how much she and Jacey had in common…right down to the belief that the happily-ever-after stuff shouldn't just be reserved for the pretty, nice, perfect princess types.

What was wrong with the wicked stepsister landing the hottie prince once in a while? Or maybe the less pretty girl who lived next door to Rapunzel, who *had* to have fewer split ends, at least. And didn't come saddled with some possessive witch who obviously wasn't so sure of her sexual preferences since she kept a young girl all boarded up for her own viewing pleasure.

"I tell you the truth, you can keep your Prince Charmings, with their white horses and their proper manners," Tori said. She shook her head, hard, trying to focus on Jacey's face, which suddenly seemed to have duplicated itself, as had everything else in the room. Then, with a wicked smile caused by an even *more* wicked memory, she added, "As far as I'm concerned, I'd rather have me a nice, smart man...who can lick his eyebrows."

Jacey shrieked with laughter, and Tori giggled, wondering whether it was the alcohol or Jacey's company that made her feel more comfortable than she'd ever felt with another woman in her whole entire life. She almost voiced her question, when suddenly she saw Jacey's eyes grow round. As the sound of their laughter evaporated, Tori was able to hear a funny choking-coughing sound from behind her. A *male* funny choking-coughing sound.

Oh, criminy, no.

She scrunched her eyes shut, then slow as she could, turned toward the door. Because fate was meaner than a miser with his last nickel, someone stood there in the doorway. Watching. Listening. Obviously having heard every word she'd just said.

And because if she didn't have bad luck, she'd have no luck at all, that someone happened to be Drew Bennett.

7

DREW REMAINED FROZEN, as stiff as a statue, while he stood in the open doorway of the library. After saying good-night to his ballet-inept students, he'd come in here looking for some privacy. Not to mention a drink.

Only, the room had been occupied, by two laughing women. One of whom had just complimented him on his oral-sex prowess. At least, he *thought* she had. Never having tried to lick his eyebrows, he couldn't be entirely sure.

Her red face and wide eyes—and the way her mouth opened up but no sound came out—confirmed it. She'd been talking about him. Referring to the incredibly erotic moments they'd shared last Sunday. He almost sighed at the pleasant memory.

"Good evening, ladies," he murmured, almost laughing at the look of panic on Tori's pretty face, in spite of his own embarrassment. Realizing Jacey couldn't possibly know who Tori was thinking about made it a little better, anyway.

"If you're back, that means everyone else is, too, huh?" Jacey said.

He nodded, fully expecting her to stay—to pick up her camera, turn it on and go right into spy mode. Instead, the woman rose, grabbed her gear and headed toward the door. She swayed just a tiny bit. "It's late," she mumbled. "And I'm beat. Don't do anything major without me, okay?"

"As if we'd forget the cameras hidden in this room?" Drew said, his voice holding an edge.

"I obviously did," Tori said with a groan. She dropped her face into her hands, her shoulders slumped.

"Don't worry," Jacey said, "those tapes are going to get lost bright and early tomorrow morning. Monahan's not going to want to show footage of a contestant mingling with the help, anyway." She gave Drew a steady stare. "I know you don't trust me. But I give you my word. Tonight's off the record. I figure I owe you that much since your first night here was *supposed* to be." Then she was gone, leaving him alone with Tori in the silent library.

"So I guess your secret's safe from the TV audience," Drew murmured as he walked into the room, closing the door behind him. Leaving the two of them completely alone.

She looked up. "My secret?"

"You know. Your criteria for the perfect man." Smiling evilly, he moved to the bar and poured himself a drink. "I believe it had something to do with his, hmm, shall we say, tongue mobility?"

"Jiminy crickets," she wailed, throwing her hands over her face again. This time she also threw herself back on the couch, until she was completely flat. "You *did* hear everything."

He poured the drink. "Uh-huh. Let me ask you something. When did you develop this, uh, standard?"

She didn't even move. "As if you don't know."

"Just checking," he said with a shrug. "I mean, I

wasn't sure if I *set* the standard or merely measured up to it."

Slowly sitting up, Tori said, "Well, since you're the one and only man who's ever done that to me, I'd say you set it pretty gosh-darn high." Then her mouth fell open. "Oh, my Lord, do you suppose Jacey's going to lose the tapes for the *entire* night, or only the parts before she left?"

Drew nodded. "I have a feeling she meant the whole night. In fact, I'm pretty sure she did."

"So no evidence to be used against us. Does that mean I can leap on you and kiss your lips off, if only to make you forget what you heard when you came in?"

"I'm afraid not. I might need them." He gave her a suggestive look. "It's not *all* in the tongue, you know."

His wicked words surprised a burst of laughter out of her. "You're bad as can be, Drew Bennett. You just hide it better than most." Her eyes sparkled with good humor.

Drew sat down on the sofa, watching her, trying to figure out why he hadn't fled from this risky situation and gone up to his room. Then he figured it out. He needed to spend some time with her, to rid himself of the memories of his horrendous evening. Even if it did put him right back on that sexual precipice he'd been trying to avoid all week.

"So how was the ballet?"

"Dull."

She nodded. "How were the girls?"

"Raucous," he admitted with a heavy sigh. "Tiffany wolf-whistled at all the men in tights and Sukie wanted to know why they don't serve popcorn at the ballet."

Her lips curled up into a tiny smile. "They don't?"

She was in an odd mood. Teasing. Glowing, almost. Then he saw the empty shot glass. *Tipsy.* "Did you have a good time with Jacey?"

She nodded, curling up on the end of the sofa. "I did. She's a lot like me, believe it or not."

He raised a brow. "Do you have vampire tendencies I should know about?"

When Tori's jaw dropped open, Drew pointed to a corner of the ceiling, where a tiny camera was recording every word they exchanged. "Gotcha," he said, knowing full well Jacey would be going over every second of this tape tomorrow morning, before she destroyed it.

"This is kinda hard, isn't it?" Tori asked from a few feet away. Her eyes said so much, told him that she felt the few feet separating them as much as he did. They might as well have been a mile, for all the emotional—or physical—closeness they could risk. Still, this was the first time in days that they'd been completely alone, without one of the giggling women down the hall, or the ever-present camerapeople spying on their reading lessons. "It's like the story with Big Brother—not the TV show, but the old story. Somebody always watching."

"That was called *1984.*"

"They didn't have reality TV in 1984, did they?" she asked.

"I think it was called MTV."

She snickered. "Jacey just came from the set of *Killing Time In A Small Town.* That was actually a pretty good one."

"I have to confess, I've never watched a reality show."

Her jaw dropped. "Never?"

He shook his head.

"Not even *Survivor* or *American Idol?*"

Another shake of the head. "I've seen enough real survivor situations. Don't really need to watch the made-up variety."

"*Joe Millionaire?*"

He grimaced. "The one where some man lied to try to get some desperate, greedy women to fall in love with him? No. Definitely not. Talk about TV at its *worst.*"

She cleared her throat. "Why does that sound a little personal, like you're very offended by that."

She'd seen that so easily, he hadn't realized how obvious his feelings on the subject would be to her. "It's an old story."

"I've got young ears."

Unable to resist the gentle warmth in her tone, he gruffly explained, "I was once seriously involved with someone who, well, let's just say if it were a case of love or money, she'd go for the money."

"That was a reality show, too."

He grunted, somehow not surprised. "How on earth anyone could really fall in love with a person who'd lie and deceive them—for money—and all for the viewing pleasure of American TV audiences, is beyond me."

"Oh," she said softly, staring at the carpet as if it had suddenly developed magical flying abilities. She didn't say anything for a long moment, then, finally, shook off the moment of introspection. Turning on the couch until she faced him, she said, "Get back to the *Survivor* stuff. I want to hear about some of your adventures. Tell me a story."

He shrugged. "You'd be bored."

"No, I wouldn't."

Glancing at the camera, he said, "Well, *she'd* be bored."

Tori followed his stare, then gave a little wave at it. "Then she can just burn this whole thing *now*."

Drew didn't suspect Tori's not-so-subtle hint would make Jacey stop watching at this point. Still, one could hope.

"Tell me."

So he did. Somehow, maybe because she was so truly interested and asked thought-provoking questions, it was easy to share some of his experiences with her. He wasn't in a glamorous field, he didn't dig for grand tombs filled with gold in Egypt, or discover new species of dinosaur. Instead, as he told her, he followed the trail of evidence that let him know about the day-to-day lives of people long since gone.

"In the future, your job'll be kind of obsolete, won't it?" she asked at one point. "I mean, all anybody in the year 2952 will have to do is watch copies of our old reality shows and they'll know exactly how we lived."

Drew groaned. "Good God, you mean Ginny and Tiffany will represent modern women?"

She matched his exaggerated shudder with one of her own. Then she said, "But look on the bright side. Everyone in the future will think men of 2004 were all brilliant, gorgeous gentlemen." She gave him a sideways glance from beneath half-lowered lashes, adding, "With the sexual restraint of monks."

"I'm no damn monk," he snapped, wondering how on earth she could think him restrained when he'd been hauling her into his arms—almost against his *own* will—practically from the first time they met.

"Which I'll prove to you about a dozen times over the very *first* day you figure out where you're going from here and what it is you want out of life."

He hadn't meant to say that, but, as usual, his emotions overruled his intellect when it came to Tori. She stared at him for a long moment, her eyes narrowing as she tilted her head.

"Oh, boy," she whispered, "that's it, isn't it? That's the reason you've been staying away from me."

"I don't appear to have done a very good job," he said, a rueful smile on his lips.

She wouldn't be distracted. "You think I'm going to be a completely different person when this is all over with. As if, somehow, changing the way I talk or the way I dress is going to change what I *want*."

"Well, isn't it?"

She shook her head and met his stare, her eyes clear, her expression somber. "Not when it comes to you."

He studied her face, searching for answers to unasked questions. "It's only a TV show, but you're still starting something that could change your whole life," he said softly. "Now's not the time for you to make any big decisions."

Tori slid closer, then closer, until there was no room on the couch for him to back away. "This *isn't* a tough decision, Drew. I want you to be my lover. Whether it's just for tonight, or for the next week. Whoever I turn out to be at the end of all this, I will never regret taking whatever I can get for as long as I can get it."

Leaning up, she brushed her lips against his. Asking. Demanding. Questioning. Offering.

And he was no longer able to resist.

Drew sunk his hands into her hair and held her

tight to deepen the kiss. Languorous and wet, their tongues met and danced in lazy, sultry intimacy.

When they drew apart, Tori said, "Was I right? Do I understand why you've been trying so hard to not let things go too far?"

He gave one slow nod.

"My God," she said with a laugh, "I feel like Dorothy in *The Wizard of Oz*, when the good witch tells her she always had the power to go back home. She just needed to learn it for herself."

"You gonna click your heels together?" he asked.

She licked her lips and eyed him hungrily. "Only if I can do it while my legs are wrapped around your hips."

TORI KNEW BY THE LOOK on Drew's face, and the groan he couldn't contain, that he had reached the end of his rope. Her wicked words had helped him, which was, of course, exactly why she'd said them. The mental picture of her bare legs wrapped around his lean hips while he thrust into her until she lost her mind brought instant warmth—and moisture—to her body.

She wanted him desperately. Now more than ever.

Lord love him for being a decent enough guy to wait until she was really ready, in every way, including emotionally. Physically, yeah, she'd been wanting him since day one.

But emotionally? Well, maybe he was right. She was already a different person than she'd been two weeks ago when she'd flown up from Tennessee. And she knew she'd have to face those changes in herself once she left here. How perceptive of him to know that.

Most men wouldn't have thought twice about taking what she'd offered. Drew Bennett, however, wasn't most men. He was different. Wonderfully, perfectly different. Smart and sexy, kind and thoughtful. Sassy and dry-humored. Everything she'd ever fantasized about having in a man but never believed she'd ever really find. All wrapped up in a gorgeous package that was hers for the taking.

Hers. For tonight at least.

For the first time, Tori felt a tingling of concern run through her body. Because she couldn't fool herself into thinking she only liked the man. Drew wasn't the kind of man you simply liked, or lusted after.

He was the kind who stole hearts. Maybe even hers.

"Tori?" he said, his voice thick. He was watching her, waiting for whatever was going to happen next.

No doubt about that. No matter what happened tomorrow, or next week, for tonight, Tori Lyons was gonna get her man. Whoever that fool woman was who'd chosen money over him oughta have her head examined because this was about the most desirable man she'd ever seen in her life.

Swiveling her body, she slid one leg across him and sat on his lap, facing him. He didn't look a bit surprised that she'd landed on his lap—again.

"Kinda like the night we met," she murmured, wriggling a bit as she moved her face closer until they were nose to nose. Then she leaned in and licked his lips, daring his tongue to come out and play.

He groaned again, rising up a little so she could feel just how affected he was.

"Oh, my," she whispered. Because he was very, very affected. "I feel like I'm gonna die if I don't have you." Her voice seemed breathy, even to her own ears.

"Ditto."

He licked at her, teasing her, nibbling on her lips. "Your room is too far away."

"Yeah, it is. But we can't stay here. Even if she destroys the tape, I don't think either one of us wants to give Jacey any kind of private show tomorrow."

She giggled, glancing over her shoulder at the camera, hoping Jacey was not watching any of this. "I'm sure she won't sit there and watch the whole thing. I bet she won't get past our conversation about the ballet."

"Maybe not," he murmured as he lightly kissed her jaw, then the sensitive skin beneath her ear. "But do you really want to risk it?"

Sighing deeply, she put her head back, wanting him to move his mouth lower, down her throat. "I think I'd risk anything if it means I can finally have you."

Her words seemed to inflame him because suddenly there were no more teasing words, no more little nibbles and smiles. Drew slipped his hand in her hair, tangling it around his fingers. Then he tugged her close for another one of those hot, wet kisses that sapped every bit of strength from her body.

"Come on," she said when the kiss ended. "We gotta get outta here before I say to hell with Jacey and her cameras and just rip your clothes off."

She leapt off his lap and tugged at his hand, nearly desperate to get somewhere private. Really private.

Drew let her pull him to his feet, but he was shaking his head. "I trust Jacey to kill the tape from this room. But once we get out of here, it's not just Jacey we have to worry about. Every other camera in the house is going to be taping us once we walk out that door, and we're fair game."

She nibbled her lip, not liking the reminder.

"There's no way you won't be seen coming into my room," he added. "And I don't want to do that to you on national television. Thursday morning was bad enough, but at least you were only there for a few minutes."

She appreciated his concern. At the same time she wanted to bash him in the head for realizing they couldn't go to his room.

"This is so unfair," she wailed. "I can't go one more night without you." To prove it, she rose up and put her arms around his neck, pressing every inch of her body against his as she pulled him down for a kiss.

He licked at her, devouring her, putting his arms around her waist to draw her even tighter. Then he pulled away and looked over her shoulder. "Come on," he growled.

Tori almost stumbled as he grabbed her and pulled her toward the French doors leading outside. "It's freezing."

He paused only long enough to grab a lap blanket, which was draped across the back of the couch. Wrapping it around her, he strode out the door into the snowy night, pulling her after him.

And suddenly she knew where he was taking her. "Perfect," she whispered, her word causing a cloud of icy cold mist to envelop her face. She shivered a little. From the cold. From the heat. From the anticipation that had been welling up inside her for weeks.

Drew didn't even seem to notice the frigid air. But he did notice her slip a bit on the icy patio. Before Tori knew what he was doing, he'd bent down and swept her up into his arms.

"Good Lord," she sputtered, even though she was starting to feel a bit like a fairy-tale princess, "put me down."

"No."

He bent his head to kiss her again, sweeping his warm tongue into her mouth as if he couldn't wait the few more moments it would take to get to the greenhouse. They shared a breath in the cold night air. Then he strode across the snowy lawn, his steps never faltering, his strong hold on her never weakening.

When they reached the greenhouse, Tori reached down to open the door. He carried her inside, then kicked the door shut behind them. They didn't need to turn on the light. The spotlights on the corners of the house provided plenty of illumination. She could see all the undisguised want in his eyes, that was for certain.

"Oh, this is perfect," she whispered, the hot, steamy air bringing instant relief to her cold face and hands.

He lowered her to stand on her own in front of him. "Thank goodness our host likes hothouse flowers."

Then they didn't say anything. They merely fell into each other, kissing like they needed each other's mouths to survive. Tori loved how he tasted, how he felt pressed against her. With frantic hands, she pushed his suit coat off his shoulders, then reached for his tie. Her cold fingers fumbled a bit, so he helped, yanking the thing off, then pulling at the buttons of his dress shirt.

She had to taste every bit of skin as it was revealed. His hard shoulder, that sharp corner of his collarbone. The hollow of his throat where dark, spiky hairs tickled her skin. Lower. Oh, Lord almighty, lower, down the man's rock-hard chest, sprinkled with more of that wiry hair. She licked and nibbled her way down his rippled belly, until she was kneeling in front of him, grabbing at his belt. The lap blanket from the library was beneath her knees, providing a slight cushion.

"I've been wanting to taste you since the last time we were here," she said through hoarsely indrawn breaths.

He didn't try to stop her, thank heaven. Tori made quick work of removing his pants, while he kicked off his shoes. Then she carefully pulled his boxer briefs out of the way. When she saw him—all of him—thought deserted her and pure hunger took over. She licked her lips, instinctively knowing what she wanted. She'd never done such intimate things with a man before, but hungered—absolutely starved—to take him into her mouth. So she did.

"Oh, God," he groaned when she covered all that pulsing, hard flesh with her lips. "Tori, you're so hot, so sweet," he muttered.

So was he. But her mouth was too full to tell him so. Instead, she showed him how much she liked his taste by drawing him deeper and deeper, sucking and licking as much of him as she could take. Still following some ancient, womanly instinct that told her what to do, she began to move, to draw deep, then pull away. The heat in the room ratcheted up and a sheen of sweat grew visible on his body. His muscles were tense, straining, and suddenly he dropped his hands on her shoulders and pushed her away.

Tori opened her mouth to protest. But before she could do so, Drew had dropped down to kneel in front of her on the blanket. "I'm not gonna come in your mouth our first time," he growled against her lips as he kissed her again.

"I did," she said through choppy breaths.

He laughed hoarsely, even as his hands continued moving frantically over her body, one sliding across her breast, her waist, then lower. Then he added, "Maybe so, but I'm gonna come *here*." He punctuated the promise by grabbing her between the legs, his fingers warm through the fabric of her slacks. Tori almost howled at the barrage of sensation.

"Then *do* it," she ordered, yanking at her sweater and pulling it off.

He helped her, reaching for her bra, unfastening it before she'd even pulled her hair free of her sweater. Then he was kissing her breasts, suckling her, feasting on her with his mouth, while he unbuttoned her slacks. Her legs went weak and the rolls of pleasure began to wash through her body. She arched against him, needing more…more pressure, more intensity. And he gave it to her, working his hand into her open zipper and under her panties. When his fingers dipped into her, she shuddered and shook, her orgasm washing over her almost immediately.

She'd barely begun to recover from it when Drew pushed her pants all the way off, dropping them with the rest of their clothes. They knelt again, facing one another on the small blanket as they touched with heated, frenzied strokes.

Had her fingers ever moved across something as warm, as hard, yet silky smooth as his body? And lordy, how could she stand any more of this sensual torture; the kisses, the fleeting caresses, when what she wanted was him driving into her hard and fast, punching up the pace the way she punched the gas pedal at the start of a race?

"I need you," she mumbled, lifting one leg. She wanted to wrap it around him and pull him down on top of her, needing him now. *Right now.*

But he wouldn't let her. Pulling away, he opened the cabinet, where they'd stashed the fluffy blanket they'd used for their reading lessons.

"Oh, yes," she murmured in approval.

He paused only long enough to toss the thing to the floor, then he was pushing her onto it. Moving over her, he pressed kiss after kiss onto her mouth, her neck, her breasts, until Tori was begging for more. "Please, *please* give it to me," she said, her voice almost a whimper. She parted her legs, inviting him, rising up to him.

He smiled at her, a wicked smile that said he knew exactly how mad he'd been driving her. "One more second."

"No, now!"

Though she tried to yank him down, he leaned away, toward his clothes. "I've walked around with one of these in my pocket since the night we met," he admitted as he retrieved a condom.

Criminy, Tori hadn't even though of that. Hadn't spared one second to consider birth control, he'd had her that hot and frantic. She watched him sheathe himself, nibbling her lip as the excitement built again.

To be honest, this slow torture was thrilling her beyond belief. "I love looking forward to things," she whispered. "The anticipation of getting something good used to keep me up all night Christmas Eve. Looking forward to what's coming is as good as getting it."

He chuckled and lowered himself close enough

for her to feel that thick weight of his erection against her curls. "Gee, does this mean you want to look forward to it, more than you want to get it?"

"No!"

"You're sure?"

"Do it now, Drew, or I swear to God, I'll bash you with one of those planters," she growled, even as she arched up to him, trying to take what he wasn't giving her.

He waited one more second, taunting her, driving her utterly mad. "I only hope after you get something good, you keep wanting to get it."

"Oh, I do...."

She couldn't say anything else because he plunged into her. Deep. Hard. Fast. Tori howled. Truly cried out at the bliss of it as he stroked her, way inside, with intense, body-rocking thrusts.

"Yes," she moaned, almost sobbing with relief at the sheer perfection of it.

As if afraid his weight was too much for her, Drew rolled onto his back, taking her with him. Tori hissed, feeling the incredible sensations battering her. She'd never done *this*, either, and absolutely loved feeling so in control.

"You're so deep," she whispered brokenly, closing her eyes and savoring the way he felt buried so far inside her body.

He held her hips and thrust up, wringing another cry from Tori's lips. "I figured you might like being in the driver's seat," he said with a wicked smile.

"I *do*," she replied. Then she began to rock against him. "I definitely like being in control of the...stick."

He caught hold of her hips, catching her rhythm and met her in an erotic give-and-take that seemed to go on forever. She rode the wave until it brought the first of several shattering orgasms, one after another, that made her entire body shake and shudder.

Her legs felt weak, and her breaths turned into pants until she had to drop down to lie on his chest. That, too, provided incredible friction. Though thoroughly sated, she *still* wanted more. Moaning, she ground against him, not believing how many wonderful, erotic things she was learning, all in one night. She fleetingly wondered if it was possible for a body to OD on sexual pleasure. But didn't much care at this point.

"You okay?" he asked, before pressing a slow, sweet kiss on her parted lips.

She nodded. "I'm a short-track driver, in case you, uh, forgot. Don't know if I've got it in me to take on these long distances."

With a low chuckle, Drew instantly rolled her over. "Well then, honey, I'll be happy to take over."

He did. Superbly. Sublimely. Until finally, when she thought she couldn't possibly come again, she reached yet another peak. And this time, she took him with her when she flew over the edge.

8

TORI DREADED THE THOUGHT of attending the country-club dance with Drew, Ginny and Teresa Sunday night. She looked forward to it about as much as she looked forward to getting a tooth filled. Or pulling ticks off her dog Ralph in the summertime.

Ticks. Fat bloodsuckers. That seemed appropriate.

Bad enough seeing the man-eaters in this house trying to catch Drew alone so they could try their tricks on him. She'd even heard Teresa whispering to Tiffany the other day that she was going to climb from her balcony to Drew's during the night and sneak in through his open door.

Tori had been tempted not to tell the woman Drew was unlikely to leave his balcony door open in twenty-frickin'-degree weather. But in the end, her better nature won out and she did.

Too bad Teresa hadn't gone for it anyway. Then maybe, she'd be sick in bed with pneumonia or something so Tori wouldn't have to watch while the woman flirted with Drew. He'd have to dance with her and Ginny, pay attention to them, and interact with them in a public place.

It'd been bad *before* he'd become her lover—in every delicious sense of the word. Now, however, she felt damn near territorial about Drew Bennett.

He was hers. Last night had proved it beyond a doubt, at least in her mind. She was crazy about the man, falling head-over-heels in love with him. She'd never have predicted it, but it'd still happened. She'd certainly been more intimate with him than anyone she'd ever known in her entire life.

And she was about to go on a date with him with two other women. Which made her want to scream. This reality show had never made her feel more helpless and frustrated than she did at this very moment.

She'd almost convinced herself to work up another realistic-sounding stomachache, which shouldn't have been too difficult since she'd felt sick about the dance all morning—when she learned something very surprising.

"We've decided to step things up a bit," Mr. Monahan said to the six remaining women Sunday morning at breakfast. "Dr. Bennett isn't going to fall in love with *anyone* if he doesn't get some alone time with her." He glanced at Tori. "So tonight will be the first of the individual dates."

The other women around the table groaned, even as Monahan and Jacey exchanged a long look, which Tori noticed.

A mix of confusing emotions rushed through her. Relief, of course. Excitement. Even a bit of resentment. Because she knew without asking that this change in plan had been Jacey's idea.

Part of her wanted to be angry that Jacey was so obviously setting Tori and Drew up for some good air-time, which, due to her promise, she'd been unable to take advantage of last night. She'd confirmed as much this morning, whispering to Tori that she'd watched as far as the ballet discussion and had then destroyed the tape.

Tori tried to remember where the oral-sex part of the conversation had taken place but was too embarrassed to ask.

Another part of her, however, was blissfully happy about the chance to get out of here and be alone with Drew for any reason. It'd been hell not greeting him with a sensual kiss this morning, after the amazing night they'd shared.

She still got all shaky when she thought about it. They'd stayed in the greenhouse for a few hours, curled up together on the blanket as they kissed, and whispered, and made slow, languorous love again. Drew had somehow managed to get her to open up and reveal more about herself than she'd ever have imagined.

Like the fact that she really *had* wanted to come here. That she *did* want to learn. That she wasn't sure what her future held or where it would take her.

Voicing the words made them real in her mind, and even after she and Drew had exchanged a soft kiss good-night before slipping back into the library, she'd been mulling them over in her head.

She'd been so excited to finally get Drew to agree she was ready to progress to the more steamy stuff in their relationship, that she hadn't thought too hard on her own realization. She was changing. And her future did look different now. Different and confusing.

Whether this completely unexpected, passionate affair with Drew lasted beyond next week or not, she had some thinking to do about the direction her life would take from here.

"So you get the hunky professor all to yourself tonight. Guess that'll be fun," someone said as Tori sat alone in the sunroom, staring out at the snow-filled clouds hanging heavy in the sky.

Looking up, she saw Robin and offered the other woman a smile. Though quiet, Robin was one of the nicest of the women left in the house, the other one being Sukie.

"I guess so," Tori replied, wondering why Robin couldn't read the wicked truth all over her.

I had headboard bangin' sex with the man all night last night, you're dang right it's fun to be alone with him!

"Would you like me to help you pick out something to wear?" Robin said as she strolled into the room and sat on the edge of the other wicker love seat. She lowered herself into it so gracefully. Good to see those etiquette lessons had rubbed off on somebody around here. "Or I'd love to help you do your makeup."

Tori gulped. Because one thing that *hadn't* rubbed off on Robin were the makeup lessons. The other woman still wore inches of the stuff on every exposed bit of her face and neck. Tori suspected Robin must have a bad skin condition or something, because Ginny, Robin's roommate, swore she even wore the makeup to bed every night.

Too bad, really. Robin wasn't exactly a beauty, but she was nice and ladylike. Not pretty, exactly. More like what her old granny would call a handsome woman. Regal. Tall and commanding respect. Plus, she had that sexy throaty voice most men liked, and a good sense of humor.

Not for the first time, Tori wondered why on earth Robin had decided to appear on this TV makeover show. Because as far as she could tell, Robin hadn't needed much making over from the minute she walked through the door.

Finally, seeing the look of expectation on Robin's face, Tori remembered her offer. "Uh, thanks anyway, but Evelyn's going to do it." She rolled her eyes. "I don't 'spect I'll even be allowed to choose my own underwear."

Robin nodded in commiseration. "Too bad. But I'm sure she'll pick out something nice." Then she leaned close to whisper, as if afraid the cameras and microphones would overhear—which they *would*—"Just make sure you go over your makeup again after she's done. She goes way too light on the eyes."

Tori bit the inside of her cheek to keep from laughing as she stared into Robin's eyes, which were accentuated by a thick black, chipmunk eyeliner ring and the longest, fakest-looking lashes she'd ever seen. "I'll remember that."

"Sukie and I are so excited for you," Robin said with a big toothy smile that dominated her lean face. "We know you're the only one who might actually have a chance with Dr. Bennett, given how…close… you two seem to be."

Tori's jaw dropped open. "What?"

Robin waved an airy hand. "Don't act so surprised. We've seen how he looks at you. And how you look at him. You're not in this for the money, are you?"

Shaking her head, Tori remained silent.

"We could tell. It's so romantic." Then she laughed. "Of course, on the practical side, a million dollars *would* provide a very nice honeymoon."

A million dollars. The prize for getting Drew to say he loved her by Wednesday. Tori had nearly forgotten about it. She'd been so focused on the other women trying to get her man that she'd lost sight of *why* they were trying to get him.

"The money isn't important."

Robin gave a sad-looking nod. "I know. That's what makes it so funny. You're the one who's got a real shot at it, and you don't care about the prize. While everyone else wants nothing but the money and he won't give them the time of day."

Tori noticed an obvious omission. "What about you? What are you after?"

"Not him," Robin said quickly.

"Good," Tori said, feeling slightly relieved that at least one woman here wasn't after Drew. "But that makes you the only one."

Robin reached over and covered both of Tori's clasped hands with one of her own. "It's okay, sweetie, he has never once looked at anyone else here with the pleasure he always shows when you're around."

"Thank you," Tori said, genuinely touched by Robin's niceness and support.

Robin squeezed her hands, then pulled away and sat back in her own seat.

"So," Tori said, "what do you want from this experience, if not the big prize?"

Robin crossed her legs and draped one long, elegant arm across the back of the small love seat. "I'm after exactly what I was after when I first came here, before we learned anything about the secret agenda and the bonus."

Tori raised a brow. "You mean, you really just want to be named lady of them all and go to some party?"

Robin nodded. "Just because they added Dr. Bennett as a carrot doesn't mean the original prize is no longer up for grabs. And I want to win it."

Judging by the sincere expression, Tori had to believe she meant it. "I guess you would get some really nice clothes and jewelry."

Robin waved that off. "The acknowledgement would be enough for me, even without the prizes. I was always the weird kid in school, looked down on, never attractive enough. Picked on. This would change all that."

Tori didn't think being called a lady by a bunch of TV people would suddenly make crappy high-school memories go away, but she didn't want to burst Robin's bubble.

With a throaty laugh, Robin added, "Though to be honest, the jewelry would be nice, too."

"Not to mention the Manhattan shopping spree," Tori pointed out.

"Exactly."

They both laughed together, and Tori realized this was the third woman she'd met here in Vermont whom she actually liked. Funny. She'd always assumed she just wasn't the type who could get along with other women—or that she needed to—since she'd never had any real girlfriends growing up. Or in her adulthood. She'd assumed the choice had been hers and that she wasn't missing anything.

Now she had to wonder if she'd been wrong. Maybe being surrounded by men—at home, at work, on the circuit—had made her the one hardened to female friendships. Perhaps she'd been unapproachable, too rough and rowdy for women to reach out a hand in friendship to for fear of being rejected, ignored. Or slugged. A few weeks ago, Tori *would* likely have ignored such a gesture, or not even recognized it. Now she feared she'd greatly miss these friendships when she returned home.

Her eyes were suddenly opened in yet another area of her life. Another experience she'd never missed, having never known it, but now knew she didn't want to lose. She liked having friends. As much as she liked learning, and dressing a little nicer, and using her brains instead of her hands for a change.

Which brought her full circle to the mental debate she'd been having before Robin had entered the room. Who, exactly, was she going to be next week when she left here?

More importantly, who exactly did she *want* to be?

Before she could give the matter any thought, she saw Robin rise from her seat, looking over toward the door.

She knew without asking who stood there. The smile on the other woman's face clued her in. But so did Tori's own physical reaction. The air grew thicker. Warmer. Her skin started to tingle. Only one man had ever made her react like that.

"Hi, Professor," Robin said, "I was just leaving."

And, God love her, she did.

"Hi," he said softly after Robin had left the room. He walked over and took the seat the other woman had just vacated.

"Morning," she said softly, not quite able to meet his eye.

They'd been so incredibly intimate just hours before. This man was her lover, for heaven's sake, he'd touched her in ways she hadn't been sure were possible, much less legal. He'd given her more pleasure in a three-hour period than she'd ever had in her whole entire life.

Yet now, she couldn't even look at him.

It's the cameras. Yes, the fact that those little peeping eyes were watching their every move had her completely on edge. Because if she gave him her full attention, no way could she hide her feelings, her reactions, her longing for more. Not from him. Definitely not from TV-watching America, who she was ready to send straight to hell by this point.

"Tori, is everything okay?" he asked, leaning forward in his seat to drop his elbows on his knees.

She nodded.

"What are you doing?"

She shrugged.

"This somehow seems familiar. Are you waiting for me to shut up for any particular reason this time?"

Finally looking up, she saw a twinkle in his eye and knew he was referring to their very first conversation. That night in the library, when she'd wanted him to stop talking and just keep looking at her. All hungry and handsome and fascinating.

A reluctant smile curled her lips up. "No, I just find I get a little tired of watching every word I say because of the cameras."

He followed her pointed stare, then frowned. "I have a feeling these tapes will be edited before they air on television."

"They'd better be," she said with a definite roll of her eyes. "Unless Mr. Mueller wants to pay a lot of fines to the TV government people. That Janet Jackson thing can't hold a candle to the way Ginny's been letting them fly the past two weeks."

"Fortunately, I've missed most of those incidents."

His deep chuckle brought a warm sensation to Tori in spite of the chilly morning. Lordy she liked being with this man.

Teasing him, she said, "Most men wouldn't mind so much."

"I'm not most men, in case you haven't noticed."

"Oh, I've noticed." She met his dark-eyed stare. They looked at one another for an endless moment, saying a thousand things, each one of them answered. They relived last night, every second of it, all in a heavy silence that the camera crew could interpret any way they wanted.

It was torture, really. A morning-after in front of the whole bloody world. But as the moment lengthened, Tori almost began to enjoy it. She got a little shivery thrill, sharing this secret with him, the rest of the world be damned.

"So have you been doing anything interesting the past few days?" he asked, giving her a look of such innocence it nearly made her burst into laughter. That was likely what he'd intended, to playfully torment her, knowing she couldn't respond.

She could play his game. "Oh, not what I'd call interesting, really."

His brow shot up. "No? Nothing enlightening or exciting going on? I can't imagine that."

"It's been terribly dull."

"Dull?" He practically wore his offense on his face. The man was fun to tease, if only to give the naughty part of him more chances to come out and play.

"Shew, I've had more fun changing out a tranny in the pits than I've had around this place." Giving an exaggerated yawn, she stretched her arms out to her sides, knowing the move was pulling her turtleneck sweater even tighter against her body. He noticed. She saw him swallow visibly. But that was his only reaction.

"Well, I can imagine working on cars is exciting for you." Then he lowered his voice. "But maybe not as exciting as racing. Being in the driver's seat, in complete control." An evil smile warned her one second before he added, "Handling the *stick.*"

Oooh, the wicked man. Her body shook, from top to bottom, at the mental pictures his words put in her head. Her tummy started rolling over, and heat dropped down to rest between her legs. She throbbed there, her corded slacks suddenly feeling too tight. Uncomfortable.

If only to get even, to make him sweat a little, too, she replied, "I'd say that depends on the stick. Some of them don't have the right feel." His eyes flared but he remained silent. "It has to be the perfect size, just thick enough to fit into my…" She licked her lips provocatively before concluding, "palm."

Drew's face reddened as he mentally substituted the word she wanted him to imagine. *Mouth.* How perfectly he'd fit into her mouth. She never could have imagined how much she'd like doing something so blatantly carnal and her whispered words told him so.

He drew in a deep breath. She watched his hand, resting lightly on the seat beside him, curl into a fist as his muscles visibly tensed. Oh, yes, she was definitely getting to him.

But he, apparently, wasn't crying uncle just yet. "Hmm, I never thought about it that way. About it fitting into your…palm. Seems to me there should be other criteria for how well it works. Maybe making sure it has stamina. Staying power. And that it's *long* enough."

She sucked her bottom lip between her teeth, almost groaning, almost laughing. "Oh, yes, length and breadth are both important. But it's the smooth movement of it that matters more than anything else."

Nodding thoughtfully, he murmured, "That makes sense."

She thought they were done torturing each other, that they'd both scored a few hits and would stop this sensual torment. She should have known better.

"So I guess you have to keep it really well lubricated," he said, his tone light. "To make sure it moves smoothly."

Tori coughed into her fist as she choked on her own breath. Oh, she was going to get him for this. Definitely get him. Closing her eyes briefly, she managed a nod. "Yes. Right. Absolutely. Lubrication is important." Then, raising a brow she added, "As, of course, is having an expert in the driver's seat."

His jaw clenched. "You saying you're an expert? That'd take a lot of experience, with a lot of…equipment…wouldn't it?"

"Not necessarily a *lot*."

"How much?"

"Enough."

"*Dozens* of sticks?"

Dozens? Criminy, did he think she was some kind of track ho? "No."

"Tens?"

She shook her head. Finally, showing mercy, she admitted, "Maybe it only takes one or two for someone to find the perfect match."

He stared into her eyes and she didn't flinch, letting him see the truth she was trying to convey. No, he hadn't been her first, but he hadn't been much beyond that, either.

Finally, a pleased look softened his expression. "That sounds reasonable."

"Glad you approve. Not that it's, you know, really up to you."

"Correct," he admitted. "As long as you acknowledge that now, having found the perfect ride, it'll be the only one you ever want to race again."

WHEN SOMEONE KNOCKED on his bedroom door late Sunday afternoon, Drew's thoughts immediately turned to Tori. He'd been ready to strangle her, or jump on her, when she'd so playfully taunted him earlier in the sunroom. Even the presence of the cameras might not have been enough to keep him from touching her. But Sukie and Ginny's arrival had been. He'd barely given Tori his not-so-subtle hint that he might not have been the first man in her life but he was damn well going to be her last, when they'd burst into the room.

Drew had made a quick excuse and left, praying none of the women—or the camera—noticed that his tailored trousers didn't fit quite so neatly across his crotch as they were supposed to.

Hoping to see Tori's smiling face, he answered the knock without even asking who was on the other side of his door. So he had to smother his quick sigh of irritation when he opened it to find Niles Monahan instead.

"I'd like to speak with you," the man said.

Drew crossed his arms and leaned against the doorjamb, not inviting the other man in to sit in the small sitting area adjoining his room.

Something about the director really got on his nerves. He was a sneaky little bastard, you could see it in his nervous eyes and his constantly moving hands. Drew wasn't risking going off-camera with this guy. He trusted him as far as he could throw him and wanted everything *on* the record.

"Okay, talk."

Monahan sniffed. "I thought you should know, there's been a change in plans for this evening."

Drew immediately tensed. If Tori had backed out, he'd find a reason to, as well. She was the only reason he wanted to go on this ridiculous country-club field trip. Frankly, he couldn't care less about what happened on the set of *Hey, Make Me Over,* and could barely muster any interest in helping to judge the remaining contestants. His life had come into brilliant, startling focus last night, and he had a hard time spotlighting his attention anywhere other than on her. On what had happened between them. What else was going to happen between them.

A lot. Definitely a lot. Maybe a life-altering amount.

After his first botched engagement, Drew had stopped thinking about settling down with a wife, kids and a house. None of that stuff seemed as important as his career and his travels, and he'd never met anyone else who'd made him think that would change.

Now, however, he was beginning to see the possibilities. Because he'd finally found someone he thought he might truly want to come home to.

"So what's this change in plans?" Drew asked, returning his attention to the director.

"We're so close to the end, and we feel it's imperative to really put the ladies to the test. To see how they function in a social setting, one-on-one."

Drew wasn't listening too closely, he was still too focused on his thoughts of Tori. Of *them*. So he mumbled, "Good idea."

Like he cared. His heart had never been in this game, and now his mind wasn't, either. He just couldn't wait to get it over with.

Funny, he'd come here for two reasons—to raise money for his charity and to see his theories put to practical use. Not to lose his mind over a woman he'd only known a few weeks. Not to give in to the most powerful sexual urge he'd ever experienced on the floor of a greenhouse.

Certainly not to fall in love.

But that, he very much suspected, was what had happened. He was in love and in lust and out-of-his-mind crazy about sassy race-car driver Tori Lyons. Everyone else in this house could do whatever they wanted with this TV nonsense. All he wanted was to get it over with and get on with his life with Tori. Because one way or another, she *would* be in his life.

"I'm glad you agree," Niles said. "Because we've decided an appropriate test would be for the ladies to each go on a mock 'date.'"

Date. Date? His jaw stiffened. This little pissant wanted to send Tori out on a date with some other man?

Over his dead body.

"Forget it," he snapped. Then he realized, instantly recognizing the problems with Monahan's idea. "It's not like there's anybody around here for her...for *them*...to go out with. Unless you're going to hire someone, and I don't think the network people are going to want their lady fair escorted by some gigolo male escort."

Miles smiled thinly. "Of course you're right. Which is why, you see, we've come up with the perfect solution."

Drew waited, sensing he wasn't going to like what he was about to hear.

"You're a well-spoken, well-dressed bachelor. And you'd be in the perfect position to judge their performance. It's truly in everyone's best interest."

Drew was already shaking his head before the man even finished his sentence. "No. No way."

"You wouldn't be going on a real date, you'd simply be continuing the 'outings' one-on-one. Think of it as a private tutoring lesson—I hear you don't mind giving *those*."

Drew's eyes narrowed. "You insinuating something?"

Monahan sniffed again and drew a hand to his chest as he protested his innocence. "Of course not. Your efforts with these women are both admirable and remarkable. This show is going to do exactly what you hoped it would. The extreme social-makeover hit of the season."

For the sake of the charity—and book sales, he had to admit—Drew hoped so. But there was still no frigging way he was going on a date with one of the women on this show. No way.

"Your first outing will be this evening," Monahan said, still ignoring Drew's refusal. "You can go to the country-club dance, as scheduled."

Drew shook his head again, but Monahan pressed on. "With Miss Lyons."

And suddenly, Drew realized, the idea wasn't such a bad one.

Not bad at all.

9

As she'd expected, Tori was given absolutely no choice about what she'd wear, how she'd do her hair, her makeup, her shoes, criminy, even her underwear. But as she stood in front of the floor-length mirror in her room early Sunday evening, she couldn't bring herself to care. "Is that really me?" she murmured, unable to believe her own eyes.

In her regular life, Tori was used to wearing jeans, flannel shirts and engineer boots. She had one plain black dress for funerals, and a blue one that did okay for weddings. The highest shoes she ever wore were one-inch pumps. But now… "I don't even recognize myself."

The dress was gold. Simple and perfect, a long straight, tight sheath that was held up by tiny sparkly spaghetti straps at the top. It glistened all the way down to the floor, where her painted toenails peeked out from strappy matching sandals. She resembled one of the long, shiny gold Christmas ornaments she sometimes saw in fancy mail-order catalogs.

"You look beautiful, Tori." Sukie was staring at her in the mirror, smiling like a proud mama sending her baby out to prom.

Tori'd been riding the circuit for more than a year by the time she would have had her senior prom.

She'd never felt the loss much. Until now. Now she had to wonder what *else* she'd missed out on, never even realizing she was missing a thing.

"Thanks, Sukie. And thanks for being so nice about this. I thought Teresa and Tiffany were going to rip my hair out when they found out."

"Pfft on them," Sukie said with a toothy grin as she cracked her ever-present bubblegum. No matter what the teachers had tried, Sukie wasn't giving up that habit. "They're just jealous because they know they don't have a chance at getting the professor. But you do."

Chance? She'd had more than a chance at bedding him, that was for sure. But as for him falling in love with her? Well, Tori still found that part debatable. Not to mention disturbing, in light of this whole contest thing.

Because even if by some miracle of miracles Drew did fall in love with her, how long would he *stay* in love with her if he found out she'd been lying to him about this stupid competition since day one?

"You do look quite lovely," said Miss Evelyn, who'd supervised every minute of Tori's transformation like a Nazi general. Tori had been half-afraid the woman was going to come into the shower with her to make sure she shaved her legs right. "Thank heaven we tamed those wild brows of yours."

Tori winced just at the memory of the plucking she'd endured earlier.

"But I do wish you'd let me go a bit heavier around the eyes," Evelyn added with a frown.

"No, thank you," Tori said, hiding a grimace. Goodness, if Miss Evelyn thought she needed more eye makeup, she could only imagine what Robin would have to say.

"No, she doesn't need anything else," Sukie said. "Tori, that gold shadow glitters just perfectly, like your dress. You don't need any more color than the bright blue of your eyes."

Tori gave her a grateful smile.

One of the other instructors, Suzanne, who wrote some kind of etiquette column for a northern paper, entered the room, which might as well have had a revolving door for all the privacy it held. "Very nice," she said to Tori with an approving nod. "You do remember everything we discussed? Waiting for the valet to open the door, letting him help you out...."

"If he helps me out, he might smear up my cheat notes," Tori said with a naughty wink at Sukie. That was pretty much how Tori had made it through geometry in tenth grade, with all those silly theorems and whatnot.

Suzanne's eyes widened and she grabbed Tori's hands, lifting them for inspection to ensure nothing was written on her palms.

"Just joshing," Tori admitted, looking at her own spick-and-span clean hands.

Behind her, she heard a laugh. She'd almost forgotten Jacey was in the room, her camera stuck to her face like always. Turning around, she gave a little mock-curtsy for the TV audience. "Think I'll do?" she asked.

"America says yes," Jacey replied.

Her comment would most likely be edited out, but Tori appreciated the vote of confidence. Then, still feeling very saucy, she retorted, "America can kiss my fanny tonight. I'm out to have a good time."

Jacey gave her a thumbs-up, even as Miss Evelyn and Suzanne groaned.

"There better not be any fairy princesses at this shindig. My elbows might go flying if we start doing some line dancing."

This time, they didn't just groan, they actually fell into one another, grimacing in horror. Meanwhile, Jacey's eyes danced with humor and Sukie snorted with laughter.

"Wish I could be there to see it," Jacey said.

"I'm surprised you won't be," Tori said, still wondering why Jacey, as lead camera operator, wasn't the one going to the club with Drew and Tori.

Jacey shrugged. "It's better this way."

Then Tori realized the truth. Jacey had intentionally backed out, probably because she, Tori and Drew all realized Jacey had lost some of her objectivity toward them. Jacey probably didn't trust herself not to give them some privacy if Drew and Tori had a chance to slip away. Last night was the only blatant help she could give them.

Tori gave her a slight nod of understanding and Jacey met her stare evenly. Though the woman was part of the crew and couldn't show any favoritism, Tori knew in her heart that Jacey was rooting for them. Not just for the sake of ratings. And not, she believed, just for the sake of friendship, either. Jacey seemed to have something more personal at stake in this, though Tori couldn't imagine what.

Finally as ready as she'd ever be, Tori exited her room and made her way downstairs to the foyer. As she walked down the sweeping, curved staircase, she saw Drew standing there at the bottom, gazing up at her.

Her heart started rolling around in her chest. Oh, the man was glorious. Dressed in a black tux, freshly shaven, his hair still slightly damp from his shower, he was like a fantasy man out of a magazine. The kind Tori had never in all her days expected to meet, much less *have*.

But the best part was the look on his face. The hungry, appreciative look that she'd loved from the minute they'd met. Again, directed solely at her. Tori thought she could live her whole life on that look, if only she had the chance.

"You're beautiful," he murmured as she reached the bottom of the stairs.

She took his arm. "Thank you." Then, lowering her voice to a whisper for his ears alone, she added, "You looked like Rhett Butler staring up at me from the bottom of the stairs. All wicked smile and wickeder eyes."

"Speaking of wicked, I hope you know I had to go take another one of those rotten cold showers this morning after I left you in the sunroom."

"You started it."

"Yeah, I plan to finish it, too."

"Gonna bribe the cameraman?"

"Maybe we could drug him."

"Or just run like hell?"

His low laughter caught the attention of the camera operator, who immediately stepped closer and zoomed in. He'd obviously noticed them whispering.

"Well, Professor, I'll try not to say any more silly things like that when we're out in public. I don't want to embarrass you," Tori said, speaking loudly for the audience's benefit. Of course, for all she knew, there were microphones hidden in the flower pots that probably caught every naughty word they'd said.

"Tori, you could never embarrass me," he replied, his tone almost stern.

Again, she figured, for the audience's benefit. But it was still awfully nice to hear.

WHILE WITH ANY of the other women from the show tonight might have been an agonizing chore, with Tori, the evening was remarkable. Perfect. From the moment he drew her long, borrowed cape over her beautiful bare shoulders, until now, three hours later, when they stood swaying together on the dance floor, using the soft lighting and the music as an excuse to keep their arms around one another, they'd been inseparable.

Tori seemed to have grown more beautiful as the evening went on. She was easily the loveliest woman in the place. The changes in her over the past two weeks had never been so markedly noticeable before. She'd always been pretty, but her newfound confidence and elegance put her above any other female here.

She held herself proudly, yet smiled with genuine warmth whenever she met someone new. The soft Tennessee twang in her voice merely accentuated her charm, and she chatted easily with everyone from the chauffeur and the valet to the club president who'd come over to welcome their celebrity guests upon their arrival.

Tonight was like a perfect first date between two people who were wildly attracted to each other. Even though they'd certainly already progressed far beyond first-date stuff *physically*.

For her part, Tori seemed utterly delighted to see evidence of the fast-approaching holidays. The club was bedecked with greenery and red velvet bows, and an immense Christmas tree stood in one corner of the ballroom. It twinkled with lights and sparkling ornaments, none of which, he realized, were as dazzling as Tori's dress.

Drew hadn't given much thought to Christmas, since the estate where they were taping showed no evidence of it at all. Probably because the show would air in February, during sweeps, long after the festive season was over. People would be thinking about Valentines, not gingerbread men—except, of course, for the grand finale episode, when the lady of them all would attend her Christmas Eve ball in New York.

The delight in Tori's eyes and the way she nearly bounced on her toes as she talked about her favorite holiday traditions merely made the entire night that much more perfect. It was almost too easy to forget the cameraman, or the interested people all around them, who knew full well that a reality show was taping in their midst.

"I wonder what on earth all these people are thinking," Tori said softly as they danced, as if she'd read his thoughts.

Then again, considering they were being whispered about by practically every person in the place, maybe it wasn't so surprising. "I have no idea. Maybe they're thinking that we're a runaway royal couple, mingling with the commoners for an evening."

She rolled her eyes. "No fairy-tale princesses for me, thankyouverymuch."

"You look like one," he said, staring into her eyes to convince her of his words.

"Maybe Cinderella."

"She was my favorite."

"Mine, too." Smiling, she tucked her head back

onto his shoulder, and her body even tighter against his, letting him lead her.

Drew wasn't much of a dancer. He'd certainly never had lessons. As a kid, food had been much more of a priority for him and his sister than Boy Scouts, sports, dance lessons or anything like that. And the biggest social events he'd attended in recent years had been around huge bonfires with tribal leaders in foreign countries. The dancing hadn't much resembled this.

Somehow, though, he and Tori made it work. They were perfectly in sync, every turn, every dip, every step.

Like making love while fully clothed.

"We have an audience," she said after the music changed, segueing into another slow, sultry number that kept them there, swaying, alone in the world they'd created.

"Uh, no kidding," he said with a chuckle, glancing at their ever-present chaperone, Sam, the cameraman.

"I meant *other* than the camera."

Following her stare, he noticed many of the other partygoers watching them from around the dance floor. Then he shrugged. "They know we're part of a reality show." Rolling his eyes in disgust, he added, "They probably think it's one of those ridiculous dating things where perfect strangers try to make other people fall in love for the sake of money or greed. That's the absolute dregs of the reality-show world."

Tori shivered a little, and Drew noticed someone had opened a door leading to an outside patio. He drew her closer. "You okay?"

She nodded, not saying anything, just burrowing closer to him. He kissed her temple, for once not giving a damn what the TV audience would make of it two months from now. "You warm enough?"

Another nod. Then after a long pause, she took a deep breath and looked up at him with a smile.

"What's on your mind?"

"Dancing. I had a feeling I was going to like your kind of dancing in public."

"My kind of dancing?"

"Uh-huh. Proper and acceptable. But still kinda wicked, like making out while upright, only without the kissing."

"I was just thinking the same thing," he admitted. Then, remembering their impromptu dance lesson last Sunday in the greenhouse—as she obviously was—he added, "I'd like to try your kind of dancing sometime, too."

"Maybe you'll come visit me in Tennessee and come to the honky-tonk with me some night."

Drew pulled away slightly to stare down at her. "Tennessee? You really think that's where you'll be?"

He was asking her more than that—much, much more. Judging by the sudden confusion in her eyes, she knew it, too.

"I don't know," she said softly. "I don't know much of anything these days."

"You'll know. And I'll be right there beside you when you figure out where you want to go when you leave this place. It'll be forward, I have no doubt about that. You're too strong to take a step back."

"I don't feel very strong." She nibbled her lip, not even looking at him as she added, "Besides which, you and I are so different, from different worlds. I don't think we should even think about where we'll be a week from now. Anything can happen before then."

She frowned, looking troubled as she added, "Who knows how you'll be feeling about me when this is all over with, everything finished and in the open."

Drew didn't understand her, but he certainly heard the concern in her voice and felt the tension in her suddenly stiff body. "That's ridiculous. And our worlds are not as different as you seem to think. I'm not who you think I am." He hadn't confided in her yet about his own childhood, which had probably been every bit as rough as her own. Now didn't seem the time or the place for that. They would, however, have the conversation soon. Once they were out of the TV business.

Tori said something else, in a low voice that he almost didn't hear. "Maybe *I'm* not who *you* think I am."

He tilted her chin up, forcing her to look him in the eye. "Tori, what are you trying to tell me?"

Her mouth opened, but no sound came out.

"Is there something I need to know about? You can tell me anything…unless it's that you're a guy in drag or something." He'd been teasing her to make her smile, but she didn't. "Uh, I was joking. Now talk to me."

She hesitated again, but this time, took a deep breath, as if about to speak. But before she could say a word, they were interrupted by Sam, the camera operator, who stepped so close with the camera he nearly hit Drew's arm.

Drew shot him a glare, watching him exchange one long look with Tori. Then he stepped back. And the moment was lost. Whatever she'd been about to say, her lips were tightly closed now.

Tori's evening had been pure magic, every minute of it, right up until they'd started talking about the re-

ality show. For a few hours, in his arms, beneath the
Christmas garland and the wreaths and the mistle-
toe, she'd been able to forget how they'd met, why
they'd come together. Even Sam's presence hadn't
distracted her too much until that moment, that one
moment when she'd been ready to admit the truth to
Drew. The words had spilled up to her lips before
she'd even had a chance to think about the repercus-
sions. She wanted him to know that *he* was the target of one of those schemes he'd been talking about
in disgust.

Now more than ever, she knew he was not going to
react well when he found out the truth. Burt Mueller
would be lucky if Drew only sued him…. He'd probably be tempted to get violent on the man. How he'd
feel about *her*, she didn't even want to think about.

But it appeared she had longer to think about it.
Because Sam had obviously overheard and realized
what she was about to do. His pointed stare had
warned her not to, and the opportunity had been
lost. The evening hadn't presented another one. Oh,
okay, it *might* have, but Tori was too chicken to really
look for it.

She didn't want this to end. Not now. And she
very much feared that when she told Drew the truth,
it would end. Maybe not entirely, but she'd sure as
heck kill any trust the man might have in her. He'd
been burned once by a woman who wanted money,
which might make him not forgive her at all.

So for tonight, she planned to take what she could.
To build up lots of pleasant moments for the memory
box in her head. Just in case that was all she ever had.

Later in the evening, as the party began to get a little more raucous and filled with holiday spirit…or

spirits, at least...Drew went over to the bar to get them each a drink. Tori saw him slip the bartender some money and then tip a waiter. She watched curiously as the bartender made a drink—adding a liberal amount of alcohol—and handed it to the waiter.

"What are you up to?" she asked Drew when he returned and handed her a glass of red wine. Tori wasn't much of a wine drinker, but this dark red stuff tasted pretty good. Put her in mind of Christmas, too, with its rich burgundy color, and that was fine with her.

"Just thinking Sam might need to wet his whistle," Drew replied easily. The twinkle in his eye gave him away.

"You trying to get the cameraman drunk so he won't follow us?"

"That's the fourth drink I've had sent over to him."

Bringing her hand to her mouth to cover her giggles, Tori asked, "So where exactly do you plan to go once he's passed out...uh, *distracted?*"

"You'll see."

As it turned out, she didn't have long to wait. Sam, a large man who'd already broken out in a sweat in this stuffy room while he lugged his heavy camera around, downed the glass shortly after the waiter handed it to him. Five minutes later, while Tori and Drew sampled a bit of heavenly cheesecake, they saw Sam put his camera down on an empty table and lower himself into a chair beside it.

"Nearly midnight," Drew said, not hiding his amusement. "Took less than I'd expected, given his size."

"You bad man, you."

"Come on."

He took the small plate out of her hand, but Tori managed to snatch another bite of cheesecake with her fingers. She popped it into her mouth, licking her fingertips. Drew noticed, of course, and gave her a mock frown. "Suzanne would be fainting right about now."

"Suzanne needs to get a life," Tori retorted. "Or get laid."

Fortunately, the music was as loud as the laughter, so no one overheard as they made their way around the edges of the dance floor. As they reached the exit, Drew glanced back at the cameraman. "Still down," he murmured approvingly.

Once out of the banquet room, Drew took Tori's hand and hurried her down a long carpeted corridor. A few people stood outside the coat check and he slowed his pace, nodding pleasantly as they walked by. They might have been touring the place…if not for the sexual energy snapping so strongly between them she felt sure they were going to start a fire.

As if reading her thoughts, he paused long enough to pull her into his arms. She threw hers around his neck, holding him tight as he lifted her right off the floor to kiss her until she couldn't breathe, couldn't think, couldn't move. She just hung there, letting him support her while he kissed the living daylights out of her.

Voices farther down the hall finally made him pull away. He lowered her to her own two feet, slowly, so her whole body rubbed against his during the long, sultry slide down.

"Oh, God, I want you so much," she whispered, letting him hear her urgency. Her frenzy.

Taking his hand again, she started pulling him

along, heading for the ladies' room, which had a nice big, comfortable lounge area, including a sofa.

"The ladies' room?" he asked, laughing but also looking hopeful.

"Wait here." He did as she asked while she went inside and scoped the place out. It was completely empty, silent and cool—and even a little bit eerie with its black fixtures and black-and-white tiled floor.

Best of all, the entrance had a lock. One that locked from the inside. Opening the door, she found Drew standing right outside, gazing up the hall on the lookout. Tori grabbed his lapel and yanked him in, kissing the surprised laughter right off his lips.

A quick snap secured the lock. A quick yank undid his bow tie. A few flicks of her fingers and his shirt was coming off. A few more and his pants followed.

"You've been making me crazy all night," he said hoarsely as he reached around her to unzip her dress. Though urgent, he was careful when lowering it, protecting the delicate fabric. In spite of the consuming want driving her every move, Tori was still coherent enough to appreciate that sweetness about him.

He was a gentleman.

But right now, the last thing he needed was a lady.

"Take me, Drew," she whispered as her dress fell away.

He stared at her, from her hair—which had loosened and fallen from its elaborate do—down her throat, her shoulders, over her bare breasts. Farther, to the tiny gold panties, then the thigh-high stockings.

The hunger on the man's face made the first moments after they'd left the house—when she'd thought her private parts were going to freeze off—completely worth it.

He lowered his mouth to hers again, this time slowing the kiss, tasting every surface; the softness of her tongue, the sharpness of her teeth. She moaned, low, deep inside, tilting her head farther so their tongues could dance and mate.

"Wait," she whispered against his lips, stepping back to separate their bodies by an inch or so. Far enough for her to work the panties down her hips and let them drop to the floor.

The stockings—and the high-heeled gold sandals—she left on.

"You are utterly stunning," he said through a tight-sounding throat. "As pagan and seductive as any tribal goddess I've ever imagined."

Oooh, she liked that image. Liked him gazing at her with that appreciation—and hunger, while looking very much the adventurer she imagined him to be in his travels.

Then his hunger faded. He dropped his head back with a moan and ran one hand through his hair in frustration. "Oh, my God, I didn't stock these pockets."

It didn't sink in at first. Then she realized what he meant. He hadn't brought any condoms.

"I don't suppose this is the kind of place that provides them in the men's room," he added.

"Wanna dash across the hall real quick to find out?" she asked, eyeing him and wagging her brows.

He moved closer, towering over her as he growled, "How can you find this funny?"

Tori nipped at his chest, toyed with one of his flat nipples until it puckered between her fingers. And until he hissed. "Maybe," she finally replied, "because I *stocked* my purse?"

He looked up. "There *is* a God."

Tori had dropped her tiny handbag on the sofa. As she reached for it, she sent up a mental thanks to Sukie, who'd made her take a handful of condoms…just in case. Tori had never expected to need them, but she'd left one in her bag…again, just in case.

Drew didn't need any more urging to continue. She barely had time to reach into the bag and pull out the little packet when he picked her up and lowered her to the sofa. He kissed her, long and sweet, as his hands moved over her body, bringing her to rapturous peaks of pleasure.

He seemed to like the feel of the stockings, because he took delight in stroking her thighs, rising higher and higher, toward the elastic. And above it. But only to tease her, to scrape his fingers across her curls until she clenched and shivered in anticipation, only to move away again.

"More, please," she whispered.

"There are no planters handy for you to bash my head in with," he said as he lowered his mouth to her breast. His tongue flicked out to scrape across her nipple, and she arched her back, giving him more access. He did as she silently demanded, sucking it deep into his mouth until the sensation traveled throughout her body, increasing the throbbing between her thighs.

"I don't feel the need to threaten you tonight," she managed to whisper between choppy breaths. "But you should remember, I do believe in an eye for an eye." Giving him only a second's warning with one evil grin, she pushed him over and moved on top of him. "And a torment for a torment." Then she began to move her lips and hands over his body, delighting in tasting his skin, feeling his strength and his warmth.

"I love doing this with you," she murmured as she kissed a trail across his chest, tasting the ripples of muscle with her tongue.

"That makes two of us."

Finally, unable to take any more, she pulled away and tore the condom open. Drew watched with fire in his eyes while she sheathed him, probably expecting her to keep control. But she didn't want it. She wanted him to ride her this time, slow and deep and strong.

Lying back, she pulled him on top of her, parting her legs and whispering, "Make love to me now."

He did, sliding into her slowly, carefully, again building that pleasure until she could only purr at how good it felt. He continued his leisurely pace until buried completely inside her, kissing her deeply all the while.

They continued like that. Giving and taking. With wet kisses and languorous strokes. Tori whispered things. How much she loved what they did together. How amazing he made her feel. How she never wanted it to end.

He whispered something back. As the passion overwhelmed them and they rode out their climaxes together, she had a hard time focusing on what he'd said. But her heart kept telling her she already knew. His words had imprinted themselves somewhere on her subconscious. *I've fallen in love with you, Tori.*

Her body soared, spiraling with pleasure like she'd never experienced and all her emotions sparked in reaction to what she felt and what she thought those whispered words had been. But her mind got the full picture. And knew she'd now reached the end.

His words meant a million dollars. But she also realized that in the long run they meant losing *him.*

10

As Drew could have predicted, Teresa and Tiffany were both eliminated Monday morning. That left Robin, Sukie, Ginny and Tori in the house, the final four competing for the grand prize.

He didn't have any doubt that Tori would win it. Everyone last night had been amazed by the change in her. Even Monahan had approached him Monday night, telling him he'd gone over the tapes from the dance and had been amazed by Tori's grace, beauty and the way she'd charmed everyone she'd met.

He also asked where Drew and Tori had disappeared to during the brief time Sam had lost sight of them. Drew had simply said Tori'd needed some air. Not caring what Monahan made of the fact that it had probably been only ten degrees at midnight. Nor that when they'd returned to the party, Tori's hair was down and loose around her shoulders. Not to mention that she looked like a woman who'd just been well and truly *done*.

The curiosity among the crew, and the rest of the cast, didn't bother him a bit. But it appeared to bother her. Tori had gone back to avoiding him, not showing up for their private lesson, not even coming to his current events class. And when they did run into one another, she'd avoided his eye.

He really needed to do something about that—to convince her she had nothing to be embarrassed about. So they'd made crazy, loud love in a public restroom. And so there'd been a couple of wide-eyed old broads waiting in the corridor when they'd finally unlocked the door and come out.

None of that mattered. Not compared to what they shared. What they felt.

At least, what *he* felt. To his best recollection, he'd been the only one making any serious statement of feelings. He'd told her he loved her. Yeah, it'd been in the height of sexual pleasure, and some men would have blown it off as the heat of the moment. Drew, however, had been prepared to admit it in the cold light of day. But Tori hadn't even asked. Never mentioned it, not there while they lay naked on the sofa. Nor while they dressed. Not during the rest of the dance or the limo ride home.

Even more surprising, when he tried to broach the subject, to assure her he hadn't just been blowing smoke because of their physical relationship, she'd changed the subject. Not too discreetly, either.

It was as if she didn't want to know how he felt about her.

"Ridiculous," he told himself Tuesday morning as he came downstairs for the day. She wanted to know, just not publicly. He could understand that, and was fully prepared to wait until they were out of here before confronting her about his feelings— and her own, which he suspected were the same.

She'd hinted at her concerns over their differences, their backgrounds and lifestyles. He could understand that; after all, he hadn't had a chance to convince her how very much they did have in common.

The loss of a parent as a child, instability, lack of money. But they'd talk about that soon.

"Professor, I'm afraid we have a bit of a problem," Niles Monahan said as he spied Drew at the bottom of the stairs.

Drew stiffened, knowing from past experience he wouldn't like hearing about any of the director's problems—or solutions. "What is it?"

"Well, it is snowing hard out there. You were supposed to have private dates...." The director swallowed hard, rushing to clarify. "I mean outings, with all the remaining contestants. But since Sukie was too sick last night, we're already one behind. We'd planned for you to have lunch out with one and a dinner with another tonight. But that still leaves one out. We discussed adding an intimate breakfast with the fourth girl tomorrow, but we really want the elimination to the final two to take place before that so the last day of taping will be devoted entirely to you and the last two girls."

The man was talking fast, as if nervous, and Drew could figure why. No matter what the hell the director called it, these little "outings" looked like dates, smelled like dates and were, for all practical purposes, dates. That and the way the director had said the last days would focus on the girls and *him* really put his back up.

Then he looked out the window and saw the snow falling, steady and thick, and realized the director did, indeed, have a problem. Drew smiled, not about to complain if snow forced the cancellation of all of these final dates, since he'd thought the idea a ridiculous one to begin with. He'd gone on the one he wanted to—with Tori. Which suited him just fine.

"Gee, sorry to hear about that, buddy," he said. "That stuff's falling so thick, I bet the plows won't be out for hours."

Niles nodded in agreement, then said, "We have thought of something else."

Drew grimaced.

"If you would spend just an hour alone with each lady today, tutoring, dining, taking a sleigh ride, however you want to spend the time, we feel that would be sufficient for us to capture moments with each one of them handling herself with a man."

Didn't sound *too* painful. But he didn't want to let the sweaty little bastard off the hook too quickly. "You're sure the others will be okay with it, since Tori did come to the party with me the other night? She was the only one who got to go off-site, alone."

Monahan smiled his thin little smile. "Oh, I think everyone understood how unique that evening was for her, especially since Sukie and Robin did go to the ballet with you. But to make up for it, we thought we'd let the four ladies dress for dinner this evening and make a special night of it right here in the house."

Him with four dressed-up, aggressive women? "Not a chance."

Niles seemed to have anticipated the reaction. "It won't be *just* you. We'll have all the instructors right there in the reception room. This will be a major test, with all of you casting your votes for which two contestants will proceed to the final round." He crossed his arms and nodded. "Should be much more dramatic this way, anyway, rather than having secret voting."

Okay. A roomful of people. That didn't sound so bad. "I suppose that could work."

"But you'll spend some time alone with each of them today, as well?" Niles prodded.

Drew hesitated, letting the man sweat, then replied, "All right. One hour each."

TORI DIDN'T MIND SO MUCH that Robin got to sit in the sunroom having a private, hour-long breakfast with Drew. Particularly since the woman told her afterward they'd talked primarily about the weather, the house and South American cultures.

She also didn't mind that Sukie spent an hour with him in the library. Sukie, who seemed to have realized Robin and Tori were the most likely to move on to the next round, had used her hour to pick Drew's brain about what she should do with the money she earned for making it into the final four.

Ginny, however…

"Relax, would you?" Sukie said that afternoon as she lay on her bed, bringing her legs straight up into the air and pointing her toes. Sukie was bored. She exercised when she was bored. She'd been exercising a lot lately, especially since she'd run out of gum and Miss Evelyn had refused to let anyone give her any more.

"They're having a nice little lunch together," Tori muttered.

"Lunch. That's it. Not hot monkey-sex on the dining room table."

Tori snorted. "I think as ladies we're supposed to say, 'Having relations.'"

"I have relations," Sukie said, rolling her eyes. "And they're all going to be hitting me up for money as soon as I get home."

Tori laughed for the first time all day. Sukie was good at brightening her mood.

So was Drew. Drew, the guy currently on a date with a wannabe Playboy bunny out to win a million bucks, who wasn't afraid to use her assets to win.

Tori trusted Drew completely. He was much too decent a guy to sleep with her Sunday night then do anything with Ginny today. Still, Ginny had to know her chances were slipping away. And desperate women… "What if she strips naked and puts those hooters of hers right in his face?"

"Then he'll suffocate," Sukie quipped. "But he won't touch 'em."

That made her feel better. She gave Sukie a smile, watching her move from leg-lifts to sit-ups.

They both watched the clock. For some reason, Sukie was now as anxious as Tori to see what would happen. She suspected Sukie had figured out something had gone on between her and Drew the other night at the party. Tori sure hadn't told her anything, but she wouldn't put it past her new friend to do some condom counting. Ever since then, Sukie had been practically bouncing in excitement, saying she was certain Tori was going to waltz out of here a millionaire.

Tori hadn't had the heart to burst her bubble. Because waltzing out of here a millionaire was the *last* thing she wanted to do. Oh, sure, the money would be nice. Nice, hell, it would be *fabulous*. But whoever the old guy was who'd said money couldn't buy happiness had been on to something. Because money couldn't buy Drew. And Drew, she truly believed, was the key to her future happiness.

It was like that Lady and the Tiger story they'd been reading in the literature and grammar lessons with Mr. Halloway. She didn't have to choose a door, but rather a path for her future. And whichever way she chose, she was taking a big risk.

"Here she comes," Sukie hissed. They both heard someone stomping down the corridor outside their room. Leaping out of the bed, Sukie dashed to the door and pulled it open to peek out. "It's Ginny all right. Ooh, she looks mad. She's slamming—"

She didn't have to finish her sentence. Tori heard the door to the next bedroom slam shut.

"Whew," she whispered. Obviously things hadn't gone however Ginny had wanted them to.

"Now it's your turn," Sukie said. "You ready?"

Tori nodded, looking down at her thickly corded slacks, her bulky sweater and the long black coat Evelyn had produced for her. "I've never been on a sleigh ride. Shew, I've hardly ever seen snow before this trip."

"You'll love it. The only trouble is you can't get naked and do the nasty out in the snow in this weather. Something's liable to freeze off."

Sukie's sassy good humor hadn't changed a bit from the day they'd arrived, and Tori had never been more glad of it. Though she'd never reached out to hug another woman who wasn't kin, she couldn't help grabbing Sukie and yanking her close. Sukie grunted, then threw her arms around Tori's shoulders, hugging her back. "Have fun."

"I will."

"Oh, wait," Sukie said, letting go to dash over to her dresser. She drew out a pair of thick gloves. "You said you didn't have any." She held them out, and watched as Tori put them on.

"You're a very nice person," Tori whispered. "I'm going to miss you when this is over."

"They have airports in Tennessee?"

Tori nodded.

"Then you'll be seeing me."

With a little wave, Tori left the room and went downstairs to meet Drew for their sleigh ride. He was waiting for her at the bottom of the stairs again. But this time, he looked more like the abominable snowman than Rhett Butler.

"You in there?" she asked, seeing only his face beneath the hat and behind the scarf.

"It's cold as hell out there," he said, taking her arm as she reached the bottom of the steps.

"Hell's hot, from what I hear."

"Okay, it's cold as…as…"

"As a well-digger's butt in January," Tori declared, the old southern expression coming easily to her lips.

"That works."

Taking her gloved hand in his, he led her outside. In front of the house, an old-fashioned looking sleigh waited. Tori'd never seen one, except in movies, and she smiled, thinking how perfect it was for this time of year. Christmas was this Saturday, and she was *finally* beginning to feel the spirit of the season. "I feel like one of Santa's helpers."

"Only with horses instead of reindeer."

"And with a human driver instead of an elf," she agreed, watching the driver hop down from his seat to help her up.

Once inside the sleigh, Tori scooted over to make room for Drew on the crushed red-velvet seat, then moved closer to him to share the warmth.

The driver placed a lap rug over their legs. "Snow's died down enough. Should be a beautiful ride. My name's Anthony, and I'm wearing earplugs." Smiling a big, toothy smile that revealed a gold cap on one front tooth, he added, "Of course, that little tiny camera ain't."

"We're used to it," Tori said, staring at the hated device carefully mounted near the base of the sleigh, protected from the elements by a decorative ledge and some Plexiglas.

"Careful not to kick it, now," Anthony said with a broad wink. Then he hopped into the front seat, clicked his tongue and tapped the reins.

Riding in the sleigh over the new-fallen snow was almost like flying. That was the only comparison Tori could make. They didn't go too fast, but they glided over the ground like a bird gliding over water, just skimming the surface and following the waves. Free and clean and fresh. Her breaths misted in front of her and snow landed softly on her face and eyelashes. She licked them off her lips, laughing at the simple pleasure of it.

"I love this," she said with a happy smile.

Drew took her hand beneath the lap rug. "I'm glad."

"I think I might actually miss the snow when I go back home. We don't get much in my part of Tennessee."

He turned in the seat a little, so their eyes met. "You really plan to go back?"

"Well, sure, what else would I do?"

His brown eyes stared into hers, serious and intense, saying a million things that couldn't be said aloud over the whistle of the wind...and into the powerful microphone of the camera. Finally, though, he murmured, "You can't go home again. I mean, of course you'll want to be with your family for Christmas."

Oh, if only he knew how she really wanted to spend Christmas. This one and every one after.

With him.

"But after that, you can't just step back into your old life, as if you'd never left. You know that, don't you?"

She said nothing.

"I mean, you're not the girl you were a couple of weeks ago. You can't go back to a life with no books and no education prospects except the Garage of Higher Learning."

Lowering her gaze, she dropped her lashes to half shield her eyes. Whatever happened, whether she stayed or left, Drew deserved to know she'd at least begun thinking about a different kind of future for herself. Beyond what she'd always planned. She had drive and ambition and hunger.

He'd given her those, too. As well as a full heart.

"There's a community college about an hour away from home," she admitted.

"That's a start." Then he squeezed her hand beneath the rug. "But there are lots of community colleges. Lots of them up north, too."

Oh, lordy, he was saying so much, without saying a thing. Almost asking her to say, but not putting it into words for the rest of the world to hear and chew over two months from now. It was so hard, so intrusive and voyeuristic. But, she reminded herself, she was the one who'd chosen to remain here. To open up her most private life to the TV world.

She'd just never imagined she'd be opening up her *heart*, too. Especially not now, when it was nearly broken, knowing she wasn't going to get her fairy-tale happily-ever-after. Not once Drew found out she'd been lying to him. He'd see nothing but the money. The competition. And he'd never forgive her.

She could stay to see that condemnation in his eyes, and fight to make him understand why she'd done it. Or she could go now and cut her losses, praying he'd forgive her over time and track her down in Tennessee.

Right now, at this moment, she honestly didn't know which she'd choose. "I didn't say I wanted to go to college," she said, forcing the words out of her mouth. "I might think about it. But I like what I do."

"Driving? Being a mechanic?"

She heard the disbelief in his voice. Of course he wouldn't believe her, she didn't even sound convincing to herself. But she pressed on. "You ever think I might like my world? Okay, so I wanted to learn. I can do that without having to change everything about myself. I like my family and I like racing and I like Sheets Creek." Gulping, she told the biggest lie of them all. "I'm ready to go back to my world. I don't know that I want to be a part of this one."

He just stared, saying nothing. The wind picked up, whistling a little as they sped by. The scrape of the sleigh's rails cutting through the new snow faded away, drowned out by the sound of Tori's own heart beating. Her blood pulsing through her veins. That voice in her head telling her she was making a mistake trying to push him away now.

"Tori," Drew finally said, keeping his voice low and intimate. "I don't want you to leave."

Oh, this was so unfair. So wrong. She wanted the moment to be private and special. Intimate. Just for her. Not for the whole cable-TV-watching public. "Don't," she said, glancing at the camera.

He shrugged, obviously not caring. "To hell with them. My private life isn't anybody else's goddamn business. They can edit this out because this stupid TV show has nothing to do with *me*. With us." He glanced down at the camera. "You hear me, Mueller? I agreed to teach here, I didn't agree to become a monkey in this damned circus." Then he turned his stare back at her. "Tori, I mean it. I know you care for me. You don't want to go. That's just…fear talking."

She stiffened. "You're calling me a coward?"

"Will you stay and prove me wrong if I do?" Then he tightened his hold on her hand. "Forget I said that. I know you're not a coward. But you're facing a choice here, one you didn't even know you'd be making when you came here just a couple of weeks ago. It's not unusual for you to have misgivings." He leaned closer, so he could brush his lips lightly across her temple. "You just can't let them drive you away. Not from me. I lo—"

"Look, a deer!" Tori squealed, desperate for a distraction. She could not let Drew say those words. Could not let him whisper he loved her. Not when that camera and the powerful microphone would pick up every word.

God in heaven, he'd just flat out said this TV show had nothing to do with him. The man had no more of a clue today than he did on day one that the show was *all* about him. And when he found out, he was going to look like a fool. In front of the world. How cruel a trick to play on a man so filled with honor and goodness and dignity.

She was so disgusted with herself she could barely breathe.

"Tori…"

"I swear it was a deer," she said, pulling away from him to sit at the very edge of the seat. She wouldn't turn around, wouldn't look at him. She couldn't, not without bursting into tears or telling him the truth herself.

Even if she did, it wouldn't matter at this point. The damage was done. There were tons of footage of him being stalked by every woman in this house—they'd get their show, and he'd still be at the center of it.

She had to convince Drew that he meant more to her than a million dollars. Had to make him truly believe she'd really fallen in love with him, for all the right reasons and not for any financial ones. Maybe, if she could make him believe that, if she could prove it beyond all doubt, he could forgive her for the rest.

And as far as Tori could see, there was only one way to prove it.

Which she intended to do. Tonight.

As soon as they got back to the house, Tori disappeared, still refusing to talk to him. To listen. To look him in the eye, for God's sake. She'd removed herself mentally from him and nothing he could say or do was going to bring her back. Until she was ready to admit what was wrong, to face her insecurities and decide what the hell she wanted out of her life, he was completely helpless.

He paced a lot that day, and skipped dinner altogether. More than anything, he wanted to march down the hall to her bedroom, bang on the door and drag her out of this house. Maybe away from the cameras, from all the prying eyes, she'd have a chance to get her head together. To figure out she did love him, damn it. And would let him admit it out loud, too.

By eight o'clock that evening, when the cocktail party was set to begin, his mood had grown even darker. He hadn't expected her to fly into his arms and say she'd forget about her father and her brothers and her whole life for him. Still, for the first time ever, he'd tried to tell a woman he truly loved her, and she'd practically thrown his declaration back into his face before he'd even been able to voice it.

Dressed in a suit and tie, since the evening was supposed to be an elegant one, he made his way downstairs to the large reception room. The owners of the house apparently entertained a lot, for there was another bar in here, even larger and more well stocked than the one in the library. The comfortable furniture was arranged in small groupings around the perimeter, with the large center area available for dancing, should the occasion demand it.

"No dancing," he told himself as he walked into the place. It was already loud, brimming with conversation and excitement. Everyone on the crew was here. Every one of the instructors—right down to a frowning Mr. Halloway, who watched them all with blatant disapproval even as he sipped from an enormous martini.

Ginny, dressed in a low-cut black cocktail dress, stood chatting with one of the camera operators. Judging by the way she kept bending closer, she knew he was staring down her dress and she didn't care.

Drew somehow didn't suspect she was going to be named lady of them all.

Sukie and Robin spoke quietly with the director, while Jacey and Sam circled the room, getting shots from every angle possible.

The only person missing was Tori.

"Where is she?" Drew asked Jacey as soon as she came within earshot.

"Who?"

He just stared until she shrugged, admitting, "I haven't seen her come down yet."

She'd better not stay in her room. If she chickened out on this event, he'd go up and drag her down here by the hair. Because in truth, she would only avoid tonight to avoid *him*.

At half-past eight, just when he thought he was going to have to march upstairs and kick her door in to get her to face him, he heard a rumble of conversation roll across the room. He was standing near the fireplace, sipping a gin-and-tonic, barely paying attention as the party continued all around him.

"Hey, y'all!"

That got his attention. That loud, twangy voice definitely interrupted his thoughts.

"Sorry I'm late. Shew-ee, I had a hell of a time finding my long underwear. Somebody musta hid 'em on me and it's too dang cold to go around without 'em. My ass about turned numb today on that sleigh ride."

Drew closed his eyes. He didn't have to turn around, didn't have to see, to know exactly what was happening. Her strident tone and heavy accent were proof enough. Not to mention the shocked silence that had descended in the room.

"Didj'all save any good food? I ain't had me a decent meal in days. Mr. Monahan, if ya only ordered finger food or some'a them slimy-as-snot snails, I might have to tan yer hide."

Finally, his eyes still closed, he slowly turned on his heel. Then, sending up a silent prayer that he'd misheard, he opened them to see Tori. Not the Tori they'd all come to know and love as she transformed into the elegant woman he'd escorted Sunday night. But the rough-edged, loud and gruff Tori who'd shown up here two and a half weeks ago.

She wore faded jeans and her scruffy black boots. Her flannel shirt hung down over her hips and was not only slightly dusty, but also misbuttoned. Her hair was slung up in a casual ponytail and her face completely bare of makeup.

And her expression was pure evil.

On any other occasion, he would have loved seeing this wild, exuberant side of her again. He'd wanted her from first glance, when she'd been exactly the girl appearing here tonight. Her clothes, her speech, her attitude—none of them made any difference to how he felt about her. He'd take her however he could get her…on any other night.

But not tonight.

Tori, what are you doing?

Even as he wondered, he suspected he already knew the answer: Tori was throwing the game.

She'd listened to what he'd said today, looked at her future from every angle and decided which one she wanted. Fear, uncertainty and lack of confidence had convinced her to go back home to Tennessee. To go back to the life she'd never thought she'd leave. This was how she'd chosen to do it.

He'd never taken her for a coward, so the disappointment flooding his body landed as hard as a punch in his gut. A pounding began in his head, the pulse throbbing in his temple. His jaw clenching, he met her stare over the crowd, not even trying to hide his anger and disappointment.

She didn't so much as flinch. She met that stare evenly, telling him without words that her decision was made.

Well, so be it. If she'd chosen to step back, to run away, he wasn't going to stand in her way. Which was why, at the end of the evening, he voted along with all the other instructors on who would leave. Ginny, of course.

And Tori Lyons.

11

THROUGHOUT THE EVENING, while Tori had done everything she could to deliberately destroy her chances to proceed to the final round of *Hey, Make Me Over* by being as obnoxious, uncouth and unladylike as possible, she'd kept her mind on Drew. On her feelings for him, and his for her. And their future. Because if she'd thought about tonight, she might have just sat down in the middle of the floor and cried. The anger in him...the disappointment in his eyes...well, the weight of them had nearly crushed her, *nearly* made her give in. But she didn't.

He'll understand tomorrow, she kept telling herself.

He'd understand, and maybe even find it in himself to forgive her for not being honest with him from the beginning. That was her hope, anyway, the one hope she'd held on to while she'd belched and spilled and slurped her way through the party.

Sukie had cried. Robin had been shocked. The only one who'd looked like she understood was Jacey. The camerawoman had stared at her good and hard, then, never saying a word, had given her one slow nod of encouragement.

That nod had been like a life ring thrown to a drowning person, and Tori had held on to it for as long as she could, using it to remind herself she was doing the right thing.

Nobody else on the crew seemed to think so. Mr. Monahan had looked like he wanted to strangle her for ruining things for him...which, she had to concede, she had. Viewers wouldn't be happy if there wasn't some romantic happily-ever-after. But she didn't care. The only way she was going to get her *real* happily-ever-after was by destroying her TV one.

But it sure didn't feel like any happily-ever-afters were coming her way as she and Ginny shared the lonely limo ride from the mansion down to a local hotel where they'd be staying for the night. Thank God the snow had stopped this afternoon and the roads had been plowed for traffic. Because if she'd had to stay in that house, if she'd had to face him, she wasn't sure she could have survived it without completely breaking down.

"You okay?" Ginny asked softly, patting Tori's hand in the darkness of the back seat.

Tori nodded, sniffing and blinking her eyes to stop the tears that had been threatening to fall since the minute the car door had shut in her face.

"You did it on purpose, huh?"

"How'd you guess?" Tori asked, her question sarcastic.

Ginny obviously didn't quite get sarcasm. "Well, you didn't much act tonight like you did all last week. At first I thought you had stage fright, like some actress or something. Then I saw Sukie and Robin crying, and I figured it out. You fell in love with the professor for real, and you know he's going to be pretty upset about this game, huh?"

"That's it," Tori admitted, not really wanting to talk about it, but unable to get away.

Ginny sighed deeply. "I've seen it in movies and read about it in books, but I never in my wildest dreams would have believed somebody would walk away from a million bucks for a man."

Tori stared straight ahead into the darkness of the glass separating them from the driver. Speaking almost as much to herself as to the other woman, she told them both the absolute truth. What was in her heart. "He's worth it."

Ginny didn't say anything for a while. Then she patted Tori's hand again. "I just hope he someday understands that *you're* worth it, too."

"So, PROFESSOR, you happy with the last two prospects for Grand Poobah lady of them all?"

Drew paused as he stood behind the bar in the library, pouring himself a drink. He certainly needed one after the evening he'd just had. Voting Tori out of here had been so hard, so bloody hard.

But it was what she'd wanted. What she'd practically demanded.

"Frankly, Jacey," he said, bringing his drink to his lips, "I don't give a damn."

The camerawoman closed the doors behind her and sauntered into the room. "Pour me one?"

Retrieving a glass, he made another gin-and-tonic and slid it across the bar to the woman who watched him in silence, her dark eyes assessing. Almost judgmental.

"What?"

She shrugged, sipping her drink.

"You have something to say?" he snapped.

Jacey lowered her glass to the bar and wiped her mouth with the back of her hand. Darn but she was a feisty little thing. Like Tori, only without the down-home sweetness.

"Why'd you let her go?"

Drew's eyes narrowed.

"Why'd you vote off the one woman who actually deserves to win this thing? Who's actually transformed herself in front of all our eyes into a damned amazing woman?"

Walking around the bar, Drew dropped into the nearest chair and stared at her. "It was her choice to go."

"She said that?"

"God, Jacey, did you not see the way she was dressed? The way she acted?"

The woman plopped onto the sofa sitting across from him, and waved an airy hand, as if his words meant nothing. "An act."

"Well, of course it was an act. She wanted to get out of here."

Jacey just stared. "And why, do you suppose, did she want that?"

Leaning back in his chair, Drew extended his legs out in front of him and crossed his ankles. His whole body felt weary. Drained. As if he'd just run a long race only to come in a split second behind the winner.

Defeat. That's what this felt like.

"I think she was afraid," he finally admitted, knowing Jacey still awaited his answer. "She realized her entire life was going to have to change, and in the end she didn't have the guts to go for it."

Snorting, Jacey began to shake her head. "You're whacked. That girl's got more guts than any ten guys I know."

"Well, what other explanation is there? What possible reason would she have for doing what she did?"

Jacey put her drink on the coffee table and leaned forward to drop her elbows onto her knees. Her expression troubled, she said, "Can I ask you a personal question?"

Warily, he replied, "Depends on the question."

"Did you tell her you love her?" Then, looking up at the camera watching silently in the corner of the room, she threw her hand up, palm out. "Wait, don't answer that."

He hadn't planned to.

"Do you care for her?"

"And this is your business because...?"

Jacey sighed deeply, running her hand over her brow, then rubbing at the corners of her eyes with two fingers. Finally, as if reaching some difficult decision, she looked up at the camera and said four words that made absolutely no sense to him.

"I'm sorry, old man."

"What? Jacey, if you know something about Tori, I wish you'd just come out and say it."

Returning her attention to him, she blurted out the last thing he expected to hear. "She did it for you. Because she loves you more than she loves the million bucks she could win if she stays long enough to get you to admit you love her on-camera."

Drew's jaw dropped. So did his heart. It took him a long moment to come to grips with what she'd said.

Jacey didn't elaborate. She didn't have to. Everything, the whole scenario, unfolded in his brain with perfect clarity. The women. The aggression. The dates. The romance.

Christ, he'd been completely set up. This was just

another variation of the classic romance reality show, only, this time, he was the sucker who wasn't in on the gag. The makeovers, the lessons, none of it mattered. The only agenda was to put him in a house with a bunch of attractive women and try to make him fall in love, with the women using every sexy weapon in their arsenal.

His fingers clenched so tightly on his glass that he feared he'd break it. Needing to, he flung it toward the fireplace, watching as the remaining alcohol sent the flames shooting even higher and the shards of glass disappeared beneath the ash.

"I'm gonna kill that producer," he growled.

"No, you're not," Jacey said evenly, "because he's my father, and you owe me one for telling you the truth now."

He didn't even stop to analyze that tidbit. He could focus only on Tori. "She knew this? From day one? From the minute we met?"

Jacey shook her head. "No. None of the women found out until that first Sunday morning at breakfast."

The first Sunday. The morning after they met. *After* their first time in the greenhouse when he'd asked Tori to stay...and she'd agreed. That, at least, was some comfort.

Jacey continued. "The women all thought they were part of a social makeover show, and they still are. You were just a...side benefit."

The glare he shot her would have made some women back away. Jacey swallowed visibly, but rose from the couch and stepped closer to him, anyway. "You're supposed to be a smart guy, Professor."

His teeth were clenched so tightly together, it was hard to get words past them. "Your point being?"

"Meaning, stop being all pissed off long enough to think it through." Her voice lowered and her expression softened. "Really think it through, Dr. Bennett. Why Tori left and when she did it."

"She probably left so she wouldn't have to look me in the eye when I found out I'd been duped and deceived by her and every other person in this house of lies."

"By which point," Jacey continued, "she'd have been a million bucks richer. Or are you going to deny that you tried to tell her something *very* important during your sleigh ride this afternoon?"

That made him pause. A million dollars. For a declaration of love. Which he'd not only been about to offer her today during their ride, but he'd *also* said to her Sunday night. Out of camera range, true, but he'd said it. So when you came right down to it, Tori had already won the game, she'd only had to prove it by getting him to say it again. On tape.

But she'd stopped him today. Given up her chance.

It made no sense. If she'd stuck around for the money, why the hell would she have thrown it away, walked away when it was within her grasp?

"Are all men totally stupid, or just the smart ones who analyze things too much?" Jacey said, sounding impatient and disgusted.

"Oh, my God," he whispered as the truth dawned with all the warmth and brilliance of a morning sun. He felt like someone had thrown him in a blender, spun him around for a couple of weeks, then tossed him out, only to learn he'd been transformed into something good. Something amazing.

A man in love. A man who was loved in return.

She'd thrown away her chance at a million dollars—a huge sum of money that could have done wonders for her and for her family. And she'd done it because she'd known that if she'd stayed, if she'd won the money, Drew would never know the truth.

That she really *did* love him.

He thought he was right. He *hoped* he was right. But there was only one way to be sure. Only one person who could tell him.

"Where is she?" he said, already striding toward the door.

Jacey hurried after him. "At a hotel in town. But it started snowing again an hour ago, really heavy. I just heard the roads closed back down because the plows can't keep up."

Drew's whole body tensed in frustration. "There's got to be another way."

Suddenly, he thought of one. Pausing only long enough to give Jacey a slight nod, he said, "I'm going after her. I'll say thank you for telling me now, but that doesn't mean I'm forgiving you for what happened here."

She nodded, her eyes suspiciously bright. That hint of brightness gave Drew pause. His curiosity getting the better of him, he asked, "Why'd you do it? Why'd you tell me tonight and ruin the big TV moment?"

Jacey shrugged. "Maybe because I've been where she is. And I want to believe the stepsister or the girl-next-door sometimes does get the happily-ever-after."

There was more, he knew it, he could see the emotion on Jacey's face. She was hurting, too, for some reason, and he sensed she had her own romantic battles ahead.

But that was for Jacey to deal with. Right now, he cared only about his own. So with one more nod of thanks, he stalked to the foyer, grabbed his heavy coat, then stormed out the front door. Heading directly toward the stables. And the sleigh.

Once he was gone, Jacey just stared at the door for a long moment, until she heard footsteps racing up behind her. She looked around in time to see Niles Monahan, panting and out of breath. "I just saw you talking to Drew, and he ran out of here. Where's he gone?"

Jacey smiled. "To get his fair lady."

TORI SAT UP LATE into the night, watching the thick snowflakes hit the window of her hotel room. They gathered at its base, rising higher and higher, until she had to stand to look outside, unable to see from her chair.

The snow was peaceful. Soothing on this silent night. Appropriate for a few nights before Christmas. She'd had a few white Christmases, when they'd gone up to visit family in the mountains for the holidays. But not any in a while.

She wished she'd have this one. Wished more than anything that she could stay here, anticipating the holiday with Drew. They wouldn't need prettily wrapped presents, not when they could give each other the gifts of love and emotion.

And sex.

Yeah, that, too. She didn't think she'd ever be able to make love with anyone else again, not after having something so perfect with Drew. He'd been joking, but he'd been right the other morning when he said she'd never want any other *ride*.

She sniffed a little, replaying that conversation— every conversation, really, that they'd shared over the past few weeks. She was going to miss him terribly.

"Please, Drew," she whispered, "please realize why I did it and find me. Soon." Then, clasping her fingers in her lap, she added, "Lord, if you can help him make it by Christmas, that'd suit me just fine."

At that moment, the jingling of bells interrupted her little prayer. If it had been Christmas Eve, she would have thought a mama or a daddy was playing a sweet-natured prank on their little ones, jingling the bells as Santa landed on their roof.

The jingle bells grew closer, louder in the silent night. She doubted anyone who was asleep would be wakened by them, but for her, probably the only soul not sleeping in this hotel, they filled her head completely.

Curious, she rubbed a spot away on the glass and peeked out. Just in time to see the sleigh come into view. It resembled the one she and Drew had ridden in earlier that day, which made her heart clench up again.

When the sleigh drew closer to the streetlight, and she got a better look at the smiling driver, she gasped. There'd been a flash of gold in that smile. "Anthony!"

Her heart went into overdrive, beating rapidly until her pulse drummed in her ears. Almost holding her breath, she peered harder, mentally urging the sleigh to move closer so she could see if it held any passenger. One specific passenger.

Then the sleigh moved.

And she saw it did.

"Oh, *thank you*, Lord, that was the fastest-answered prayer I've ever heard of," she muttered even as she grabbed for her coat and pulled it on over her pajamas. She yanked her boots on, too, not bothering to tie them, then raced out the door onto the second-floor balcony.

"Drew!" she said in a whisper that masqueraded as a shout.

He looked up immediately. Met her stare for the longest moment Tori had ever experienced in her whole entire life.

Then that mouth widened into a smile. And everything was right with the world again.

She ran for the steps, tripping down them two at a time while he approached from the bottom. When they got close enough, Tori launched herself down, landing with an *oomph* in his arms. Then those arms closed around her and he hauled her close, covering her mouth with his for a sweet, wonderful, hungry and loving kiss.

When they parted, she gazed up at him, wanting to ask a bunch of questions, not quite knowing where to begin.

He beat her to the punch by answering the most important one. "I know about the show."

She watched him warily.

"I know you were all supposed to try to get me to fall in love with you."

"Sukie?" she asked.

He shook his head. "Jacey."

That surprised her for only a moment. Then it made sense.

Frowning in concern, she asked, "Are you okay?" Not waiting for his answer, she hurried on. "Of course you're not okay. It's awful and embarrassing and humiliating and I'm so sorry I ever had anything to do with it."

When she'd finished babbling, he said, "You could have won."

She nodded.

"You walked away."

Another nod was all she could manage.

"Because you love me."

He wasn't asking. The man was stating a fact. Relief flooded through her whole body and she smiled, wanting to jump up and down and shout loud enough to wake up the whole hotel.

He understood. And miracle of miracles, judging by the loving way he was looking at her, he believed.

"I do," she finally said, her voice breaking with emotion. "I love you so much, and I'd never in this lifetime want you to think you were nothing but a dollar sign to me."

"A million dollar signs," he pointed out.

"Don't remind me," she said with a light groan. Then she cupped his cheek in her hand. He instantly covered her cold fingers, protecting her skin, warming her.

"You're worth it, Drew. I wouldn't risk losing you for every penny on this earth. I love you with all my heart."

Lowering his mouth to hers again, he kissed her deeply, hungrily, as if wanting to taste the words she'd just said. When they finally parted, sharing a few icy cold breaths, he whispered, "I love you, too, Tori Lyons. Sassy race-car driver and lady of them all, I love you for everything you are."

Smiling gently as tears rose in the corners of her eyes, only to freeze there, she said, "And that is the most perfect Christmas present I will ever get."

"It's not Christmas yet."

"Soon."

"Will you spend it with me?"

She nodded. "Have anything special in mind?"

"Oh, yes. Very special. In New York."

She suspected she knew what he meant. He wanted to walk into that ball on Christmas Eve with her on his arm. To let the producer and the director and the TV crew—and all those *watching*—that what they'd found, what they'd learned, had risen above everything and everyone around them.

The TV show couldn't cheapen their relationship ever again.

She could think of nothing more wonderful— more perfect—than to spend the evening with the love of her life, and the wonderful friends she'd made. Sukie. Robin. Jacey. They'd be there, she felt sure. The final four contestants had been invited to attend, to watch the winner be crowned. The rest of the world could think whatever they wanted. Those who knew her would understand completely if she arrived with her *real* prize. Drew.

"That sounds like a perfect way to spend Christmas."

"And you'll spend every one hereafter with me, too?"

"Was that some kind of proposal?"

"A lousy one," he admitted, his voice starting to shake with the cold. "But if I drop to one knee I'm afraid my pants will freeze to the steps and I'll never be able to get up."

She giggled, realizing that in spite of being warmed by love, it was frigging *frigid* out here.

"I'll give you a proper proposal when you're ready. After you figure out where you're going and what you want to do."

Grabbing a fistful of his coat, she pulled him close. "Just don't you stop making love to me in the meantime, mister big-shot professor." Kissing the tip of his icy nose, she added, "And my future is with *you*." Almost unable to contain her excitement, she rattled off all the plans and dreams that had been spinning around in her head for days. "I want to go to school, and live with you, and make babies with you, and be a mechanical engineer, and teach our little ones to read, and marry you, and go on trips with you to the Amazon, and see every museum and art gallery in Washington, and learn how to speak French and…"

"All at the same time?" he asked, laughing and shaking his head at the same time.

"In whatever order it suits us."

She shivered a bit, but not from the cold. It was from the possibilities rolling out in front of her. In front of them.

Endless, glorious possibilities.

Seeing her shiver, he looked down. His eyes widened when he saw her pajamas under her unbuttoned coat. "My God, Tori, you're going to freeze to death before you can learn one French word, much less make any babies." He immediately started to button her up.

"So come upstairs and keep me warm, big man," she said with a teasing grin.

"I think my entire body is frozen from the neck down."

"I think I can thaw certain parts of you out pretty quickly," she promised with a saucy toss of her head.

"I'm counting on it," he retorted, his eyes glittering and hungry. "But until my legs rise fifty degrees back to room temperature after that sleigh ride, you might have to do the driving." His tone was just as suggestive.

"I'm a good driver," she teased.

"I've heard that about you."

She walked faster, the excitement warming her as she thought of the long, sensuous night to come. In a bed. A real *bed*.

"Tori?" he said, as they stopped in front of her door, still open from her dash outside. Good thing, since she hadn't grabbed a key.

"Yes?"

"Will you do something for me?"

"Anything."

He caught her fingers and brought them to his mouth, pressing a gentle kiss there. And suddenly, she began to feel a bit like that lady fair.

Finally, with love shining in his eyes, he whispered, "Don't ever change."

12

JACEY HADN'T BEEN BACK to New York in a few weeks, so when she called Digg to let him know she'd be in town for Christmas Eve, she honestly wasn't sure what to expect. Would he welcome her? Be angry that she'd left? Be ready to end things, or ready to start all over again? Whatever the case, she was going to meet with him, face to face, and start working on the problems in their relationship. She loved the man, and he was worth any concessions she had to make to work things out.

Tori Lyons had just given up a million dollars for the man she loved, for cripe's sake. Jacey oughta be able to put up with a disapproving future mother-in-law. But she was still nervous. Because she'd left pretty suddenly and she and Digg hadn't seen each other since.

The Lady of Them All Ball was being held at a new ritzy Manhattan hotel that catered to the rich and tacky. It wasn't one of the old-school elegant establishments, which would be much too highbrow to allow camera crews from a reality show into their midst. But this one did just fine. It was gaudy and glittering, just right for reality TV and everything it entailed.

To her great surprise, her father had flown in to attend. She wasn't sure he'd even be speaking to her after what she'd done on the set of *Hey, Make Me Over*. He'd said a few words on the phone after the show had wrapped—and he'd gotten a full report from a furious Niles Monahan—but he hadn't blown his stack. When he met up with her in the lobby of the hotel, a few minutes before the ball was to start, she figured out why.

"I've got the most fabulous idea for a new show," he said, his voice nearly bellowing, as he kissed her on the cheek in greeting. "The last one might not have had the romance we wanted, but we will still crown our lady fair. And we'll get the romance next time. I've signed a former actress to be a damsel and I'm going to have men compete in physical challenges for her favor."

"Sounds stupid," Jacey said, rolling her eyes, though secretly glad he wasn't holding a grudge. She hadn't had the heart to tell him that a romance really *had* developed on the set of this show. It didn't seem the right time, besides which, she hadn't even heard from Tori or Drew since he'd taken off after her in that blizzard Tuesday night.

"I dunno, sounds pretty smart to me," a voice said. "Some women need to be *convinced* they're loved."

Digg. Oh, God, it was Digg. She'd know that smooth, slightly accented voice anywhere. Turning toward him, she saw his familiar handsome face, his dazzling white smile that had captivated half the women in America on TV last fall. He looked the same, all except for the classic black tuxedo, so different from his usual casual Hispanic firefighter look.

She'd never seen anything that looked better. Sucking in a deep breath, she threw herself into his arms. Hugging him tightly, she said, "I'm sorry I left. We have a lot to talk about. I've learned so much. I know I can't blame you for what's wrong if you don't even know what's happening."

He kissed her softly, cupping her face in one hand to stare at her with those deep brown eyes. "Welcome back. And we do have some talking to do. You won't be running out on me again anytime soon, will you?"

Burt, who'd been standing there watching them with a knowing smile on his face, stepped over and clapped Digg on the back. "Well, you know I'm counting on my daughter to be part of my next few projects. I need her help…in a few areas."

For the first time, Jacey noticed a troubled frown on her father's face, but she didn't have time to evaluate it. Right now she had to introduce him to the man she loved.

After she did, they shook hands and Digg murmured, "I don't know if I can take these long separations. We might have to do something about that."

Jacey was distracted by the arrival of some of the girls from the show, so she didn't have time to question that funny twinkle in Digg's eye, or the way he and her father exchanged a secretive look. Swinging her camera up and into action, she focused on Sukie and Ginny, who'd arrived together and were being escorted by two studs Burt had hired for the evening. Judging by the way Ginny was rubbing the arm of hers, there might be some romance here tonight, after all.

"Is our lady fair here yet?" Burt asked, whispering softly.

Jacey shook her head, zooming in on the girls as they entered the ballroom and oohed and aahed over the decorations. There were already a number of people here; invitations had been sent out all over the place and a lot of New Yorkers who'd have otherwise spent the holiday home alone had ventured out for a festive Christmas Eve.

Sukie didn't seem to mind not having won. Jacey figured she'd been shocked just to make it into the final two. They *all* had been, once Tori had removed herself from the running.

In the end, the crown had gone to Robin, by a five to one vote. Only old Mr. Halloway had gone the other way, mumbling something about not entirely trusting Robin. Since Robin was one of the few Jacey had actually liked, she'd ignored the old man's mutterings.

"Ahh, here she is," Burt said, clapping his hands together as Robin came in on the arm of yet another stud.

She looked beautiful, tall and slim and so elegant in her long sapphire-blue gown. It was tailored to deemphasize her rather broad shoulders and flatter her slim waist and hips. And she looked so happy, Jacey almost wanted to clap for her.

This reality show thing had been pretty stupid. But it had had its moments. This was shaping up to be one of them.

As the party progressed, Robin met with some of the members of the press who'd been invited. She did on-the-spot interviews, and agreed to make the rounds on some network morning shows. Then, at close to midnight, Burt took the stage and cleared his throat to make the final announcement about Robin's triumph.

The writers had written his speech, so it went off like clockwork, including his grand flourishing bow as he concluded, "And now please welcome the lady of them all, Miss Robin Calvin."

Robin was blushing, tears streaming down her face as she walked toward the small stage set up on the dance floor. She continued to cry, causing her makeup to smear down in thick black streaks as she was escorted up the steps.

"Please accept this as a token of our very high esteem, Miss Calvin," Burt said. He extended a velvet box, which Jacey knew held a sapphire necklace worth a cool ten grand.

Robin accepted it, kissed Burt on the cheek, then turned to face her clapping audience.

It was like a frigging beauty pageant, only, this time, the winner hadn't been trained from birth to always wear a plastic smile and parrot ideas about world peace and freedom. She was a real woman. A genuine, down-to-her-toes American girl who'd worked hard to improve herself to *earn* this moment.

"This is pretty good stuff," she murmured to Digg, who stood right beside her, watching, a quiet, soothing presence as always.

"Nicely done," he replied. "Congratulations."

Burt had left the stage and reached them in time to hear Digg's comment. "Thanks." He clapped his hands together, rubbing them in glee, adding, "This is perfect, absolutely perfect." Then he shrugged. "Okay, not perfect. An engagement would have been perfect. But this is pretty damn good."

Jacey smiled and continued to tape, sending up a silent little Christmas prayer that somewhere, Drew and Tori were celebrating an engagement tonight.

"Ladies and gentlemen, I can't begin to tell you how much this means to me," Robin said into the microphone. The crowd's applause died off in anticipation of her remarks. "Ever since I was a teenager, I've dreamed of wearing a beautiful gown and glittering jewels and being among all you elegant people, feeling like I truly belonged somewhere, at last."

"Schmaltzy," Burt whispered, "but good."

Jacey ignored him, holding the shot steady.

"Tonight is especially sweet, for another reason," Robin said, giving the crowd another huge smile. "Because not only can I celebrate it on my own behalf, but I can share it, with all those others out there like me, who were unfortunate enough to be born in the wrong bodies."

Jacey stiffened, not quite sure she understood what Robin was getting at. It wasn't like there had been any plastic surgeries on *Hey, Make Me Over*, it wasn't *that* kind of makeover where women got the perfect bodies with liposuction or tummy tucks.

Then she gasped, as did much of the crowd, when Robin reached up to the top of her head and pulled her own hair.

Off. Right *off*.

"Oh, shit," Digg whispered, sounding stunned.

Jacey could only nod in agreement, but there was no frigging way she was taking the camera off Robin. No way.

Because she was starting to understand.

"Ladies and gentlemen, thank you so much, but please, do allow me to accept your accolades under my real name. It's *Rob*. Rob Calvin. And I consider tonight a triumph for transvestites like me everywhere in this great nation of ours." Fresh tears rose in her...*his* eyes. "This is for you, my sisters! Celebrate your individuality. Express yourself. Be the lady deep within you and the world will be at your feet!"

The entire room fell into a long moment of absolute silence. You could have heard an eyelash fall as the crowd—the audience—absorbed the grand finale.

The lady of them all was a dude.

Then everyone spoke at once. Gasping, chattering, shooting questions at Robin. Rolling with the punches as only good old New York could.

Jacey couldn't help it. She started to laugh. And laugh. Until the tears rolled out of her eyes, blurring her vision, making it impossible to see through the camera lens. "Oh, my God," she said as she almost snorted.

"Lady's a guy," Digg said with a casual nod. "Neat twist."

Finally Jacey worked up the nerve to look at her father, who was staring, goggle-eyed, at the scene unfolding on the stage. His face was red, his mouth open but no sound was coming out. Then finally he managed to whisper, "Ruined. I'm ruined."

"Don't be overdramatic. It's a great twist."

"Which no one will ever see," he replied, still keeping his voice low as the shock kept him frozen in place. "The network will never air this. The entire production was an exercise in futility." He began to shake his head, mumbling, "No lady fair, no romance, no happily ever after, no millionaire. It's a flop. A total flop."

Jacey was about to offer comfort to her father, although she did see his point. His prediction might very well come true, the way the lame-ass networks reacted to every slightly controversial thing that came along these days. But then Digg touched her arm, whispering, "Who's that?"

Giving him a questioning look, she saw him nod toward the dance floor. She tried to follow his stare, but her view was blocked by the crowd of people, who'd surged forward to surround Robin...er, Rob. She—he—continued to hold court onstage, with a supportive Sukie on one side and Ginny on the other.

Then the crowd shifted. Jacey sucked in a breath as she saw them. The two of them. Dancing there on the floor, oblivious to the cacophony, to the mania, to the hysteria.

The small orchestra was playing the Christmas Waltz, and beneath the soft spotlights, Drew Bennett and Tori Lyons slowly danced. Swayed. Loved. As blatantly and obviously...and *beautifully*...as anyone ever had before.

Tori wore a stunning burgundy gown, velvet on the top, with layers upon layers of lace, cascading to the floor, so she resembled nothing less than a fairy princess. A perfect Christmas angel, dancing with her tuxedoed Prince Charming.

Their eyes never strayed from each other. Their smiles were intimate, their whispers for no one else's ears but their own. They didn't see anyone else, didn't hear anyone else. All around them the party went to hell, but the professor and his lady fair danced on.

They probably could have danced all night.

"Dad," Jacey murmured, sensing Burt was about to walk away in dismay to cry over his ruined show. "Look."

Burt paused, probably at first over his shock at what she'd called him. He followed her stare, then gave her a questioning look. Finally, he appeared to recognize who was dancing. "Is that..."

"That's them. We might have our happily-ever-after yet."

Ever the slave to her craft, Jacey swung her camera up to her face and began to tape them, to capture the moment.

But *not* up close. Only from afar. She wouldn't dream of intruding on their privacy—she merely let the world get a glimpse of a true fairy-tale ending. Like opening a cherished Christmas card to get a peek at what was inside, then closing it again, secure in the good tidings it had brought.

Slowly, with Digg's hand on her shoulder, and her father beginning to smile by her side, she sent a silent Christmas wish for many years of happiness to the oblivious couple, spinning away on the dance floor.

And then she faded to black.

* * * * *

*If you enjoyed MAKE ME OVER,
don't miss GETTING REAL,
the ultimate reality TV anthology,
available next month
wherever Harlequin books are sold.*

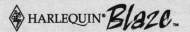

eHARLEQUIN.com

The Ultimate Destination for Women's Fiction

The eHarlequin.com online community is *the* place to share opinions, thoughts and feelings!

- Joining the community is easy, fun and **FREE!**

- Connect with **other romance fans** on our message boards.

- Meet your **favorite authors** without leaving home!

- **Share opinions** on books, movies, celebrities…and *more!*

Here's what our members say:

"I love the friendly and helpful atmosphere filled with support and humor."
—Texanna (eHarlequin.com member)

"Is this the place for me, or what? There is nothing I love more than 'talking' books, especially with fellow readers who are reading the same ones I am."
—Jo Ann (eHarlequin.com member)

Join today by visiting
www.eHarlequin.com!

Silhouette®

Desire

A compelling new family saga begins
as scandals from the past bring turmoil to
the lives of the Ashtons of Napa Valley, in

ENTANGLED
by Eileen Wilks
(Silhouette Desire #1627)

For Cole Ashton, his family vineyard was his first priority,
until sexy Dixie McCord walked back into his life, reminding
him of their secret affair he'd been unable to forget.
Determined to get her out of his system once and for all, Cole
planned a skillful seduction. What he didn't plan was that
he'd fall for Dixie even harder than he had the first time!

DYNASTIES: THE ASHTONS

A family built on lies...
brought together by dark, passionate secrets.

Available at your favorite retail outlet.